for my bro

Dick
12/23/2011

Tomorrow is Just Another Road

Tomorrow is Just Another Road

Richard Standring

Riverhaven Books
www.RiverhavenBooks.com

Tomorrow is Just Another Road is a work of fiction. While some of the settings are actual, any similarity regarding names, characters, or incidents is entirely coincidental.

Copyright© 2011 by Richard Standring

All rights reserved.

Published in the United States by Riverhaven Books
www.RiverhavenBooks.com

ISBN : 978-1-937588-03-8

Printed in the United States of America
by Country Press, Lakeville, Massachusetts

Designed and Edited by Stephanie Lynn Blackman
Whitman, Massachusetts

For Marcia
and
all of our friends
at
Pelican Point

Word Merchant
P.O.Box 153, Pembroke, MA 02359
781/293-9510
wordmerchant12@yahoo.com

Rolly,

For those who are homeless, and without much hope, **tomorrow is just another road**, not leading anywhere. Try to walk a mile in their shoes. Not an easy thing to do. In today's economic climate, there are too many people in jeopardy of losing their homes, losing their jobs and maybe their dignity.

A year ago, while vacationing in Florida, I decided to write a short story about a homeless man trying to exist while camping near a roadside park, only to be rousted by a sheriff's deputy who regarded homeless people as a disgrace to society. I wanted to interject some humor and put a face on the situation. I gave a first draft to a friend who liked it, but said he wanted the story to be longer. So, I wrote another 1,500 words to satisfy him. Still he wanted more. I couldn't see

...worked with several. The first being, Loner. Next, Nowhere to Go.

This past fall, I decided to add a few more similar stories and put the collection under an umbrella title and publish it. I know it appears to be a meager effort, but I think you just might enjoy some of the humorous incidents described. This is your personal copy. Feel free to pass it onto to some of your friends. Also feel free to comment. Since I used an editor and a publisher to review everything, you shouldn't discover too many mistakes.

And when you read between the lines, you'll discover the need for compassion for those less fortunate than we are. If you are so moved, make a donation to The Salvation Army, for they are truly helping the needy, of which there are too many.

Richard Standring

Dick

Prologue

Home is a place we take for granted. It's a place where we grew up, a place where we feel safe, and a place where the family awaits our arrival. Home is the place at the end of our journey.

Sadly, for hundreds of thousands, home is just a tent in a park or perhaps a temporary cot in a shelter, where neighbors are strangers, suffering from hunger, loneliness, and often depression. Homeless people have nowhere to go, not even an empty promise for a future. Despair and poor health are constant companions. This sad human condition is often brought about by job loss, too many debts, a domestic situation, mental illness, a terrible addiction, or a tragic event like Hurricane Katrina.

For many of these helpless people, tomorrow is no longer a challenge: It's taking it one mile, one step, at a time, because **tomorrow is just another road.** These short stories focus on fictional circumstances, some of which are humorous, to put an emphasis on their plight. Home, like life itself, is a temporary place, to be enjoyed, appreciated, and remembered.

Richard Standring

Table of Contents

Tomorrow is Just Another Road 1
Not My First Rodeo 23
Another Road 30
Sleeping in a Cardboard Box 51
Starting Over 58
Bayou Boogie Blues 65
Escaping Katrina 86
Saturday Morning Blues 93
12th Street Shelter Blues 101

Tomorrow is Just Another Road

Suddenly homeless, a man discovers human kindness along with every day difficulties while learning about life's true priorities.

"Hey, boy, want to sell that bike? I'll give you twenty-five dollars."

"No way! I'll bet you don't even have twenty-five dollars," the kid said as he slowed to keep pace with the homeless man walking beside the road. The road was U.S. Highway One, and eleven-year-old Danny knew better than to talk to strangers, particularly a homeless man with wild-looking hair and a beard. He wasn't afraid, however, because of all the passing traffic on the heavily traveled road at all hours.

"I was going to give you an IOU," the bearded man laughed. His head was bent forward and he was looking down rather than ahead as he walked. He had a backpack and a walking stick. His sneakers showed a few holes.

"You must think I'm really stupid."

"Not any more. You just proved you're a smart kid. So how 'bout I give you forty instead?"

"You might as well make it a hundred, I'm not selling."

"Yep, you're a smart kid alright. I was just testing you."

"What's your name?" Danny asked.

"Name's Will, short for Willoughby. What's yours?"

"My name's Dan, short for Danny," the boy said mockingly. "Do you want half of my candy bar? I'll bet you haven't had any breakfast." For some strange reason Danny was intrigued with the man who seemed to walk faster than most people. It was a steady pace.

"Sure. I never turn down an offer for free food." He stopped and waited for the boy to unwrap the candy bar and break it in two pieces.

At that same moment a police cruiser pulled up behind the two. A deputy sheriff leaned out the window and yelled, "What do you think you're doing, son? Get away from that man!"

Scared, Danny pedaled off, dropping the candy bar. He didn't want to get arrested.

"And you, what were you handing that kid?" the officer asked.

"He was just giving me a piece of his candy bar." Will bent over and picked up the broken pieces, putting one into his mouth and smiling as broadly as he could manage. He had a lot of experience with the law. He knew that even a false smile was better than a frown. He also recognized the deputy sheriff who was yelling at him. This one had no sense of humor and a very short fuse.

"What's your name?" the officer asked.

"Same as the last time you asked: Willoughby."

"Willoughby what? What's your last name?"

"It's just Willoughby. Don't remember my last name, haven't had to use it in a long time." *It was probably the last time you rousted me,* he thought.

"I need a last name," the deputy said.

"Okay, put down Jones." This whole scene amused him. For some reason, homeless people seemed to pose a threat to the rest of society. In Will's case, he just wanted to be left alone.

"Is that your last name or are you making it up?"

"I told you, I don't remember my last name. Is it important? Did I win the lottery?"

"Don't run that smart mouth with me! I'm the one asking the questions."

"Yes, you are. And I appreciate having someone as intelligent as you to talk with."

"Okay, get in the backseat; we're going for a little ride." The deputy hated homeless people and those with a smart mouth, like this one, sometimes drove him over the edge. He felt it was his duty to rid the community of these cockroaches.

"Good. I'm tired of walking anyway."

The deputy drove a few miles south, crossing over a bridge into a community known as Roseland. The bridge crossed the Indian River, a dividing point between Brevard County and Indian River County. Will knew all about the county borders, having crossed them many times.

"I guess we're out of your jurisdiction. Mind letting me out up there at the 7-Eleven so I can use their bathroom?"

"I'm not your personal taxi. And I'm only going to tell you this once: stay out of my county. If I pick you up again, for any reason, I'll put your sorry ass behind bars. You got that?"

"Think I heard it once before. Let's see, it's been about two months. You didn't want to put me up then either. But I want you to know that I did hear you, and I'll keep it in mind. When I see the sheriff, I'll be sure to tell him what a good job you're doing."

"Get out and keep going!" The deputy had to get out first to open the door for Will, just like a chauffeur might do for a client, since there was no way to open the rear doors from inside.

Will bowed and muttered his thanks for the lift. "Wish I could leave you a tip, but I'm all out of small bills," Will yelled after the departing police car.

The cruiser did a U-turn and sped off back across the bridge. Will thought he just might wander back later in the afternoon since he had a tent hidden behind some brush along the riverbank near a small park and public boat ramp. Once in a while a pickup truck with an empty boat trailer would be parked there and, if it was unlocked, Will could find small change and a variety of junk worth taking.

Sometimes fishermen would share their catch with him. Like the boy on the bike, they didn't regard him as a menace, just someone down on his luck and needing a handout.

Will liked this section of Florida. The weather was warmer and the Indian River ran close to Highway One, providing a lot of nice places to camp without being seen. The sea grape bushes and mangroves provided good cover from the highway. This section was sparse and had few homes. Most of the businesses were small marinas, a mobile home park, a few cheap bars, and two boat dealers. Traffic between Melbourne and Vero Beach was always heavy, regardless of the hour.

Will had to make some quick adjustments a few months back. That's when the world had turned for him. He could still remember the day it all happened. It was his forty-fifth birthday and he'd started celebrating the night before, getting an early jump on the special occasion.

He recalled waking up late because he'd been drinking heavily the night before. That's when he'd found the note propped up on the kitchen table announcing another major event. Instead of a birthday card, his wife, Cathy, chose this particular day to announce she wanted a divorce "after fifteen years of aggravation." She also wanted him out of the apartment by the end of the day. He never saw it coming.

Cathy had a good job as a beautician. But she always wanted things they couldn't afford. She thought they should have a big flat screen, high definition television and stainless steel appliances because that's what all her friends had. When Will wasn't agreeable to those purchases, she surprised him by trading in her old Oldsmobile and buying a late-model Miata convertible. Will decided she must be going through *the change* and refused to argue about it.

He remembered calling his boss to tell him he'd be late for work because he had a few personal things to take care of. In fact, he had to find a new place to stay.

"Don't bother, Will. I hate to tell you this, but now is probably as good a time as any. We're letting you go. We've had to cut back on drivers and your attendance record hasn't been all that good lately. Stop by later and pick up your check." Will remembered that brief conversation to the word.

And, when he went to the bank to cash his last pay check, he learned that Cathy had already closed out their joint account. Apparently, she'd planned ahead and he hadn't recognized any of the signs of this pending disaster.

That's how his day had started. Without a job to go to, and no home to return to, Will didn't see any reason to stick around.

If Cathy wanted to have him served with divorce papers, she'd be out of luck trying to find him.

When he was still working, driving long-haul rigs, Will drove through many interesting areas he liked. Most were in the southeastern part of the country, and that's where he was headed: destination unknown. The tricky part was he would be driving his old Ford Ranger with a cranky transmission that would soon need attention. Just how far he'd get was questionable. He planned on staying at cheap motels along the way. He was traveling light with just one suitcase. He'd look around for another driving job once he got settled.

He had driven south on secondary roads to keep his speed down. He didn't want to break down on an interstate highway. He was in no hurry and had a lot of time to think. He tried to be angry with Cathy for what she'd done. Digging deep into his memory bank, he knew he was part of the problem, yet he'd been blind-sided by the sudden decision to end it all. No argument, no discussion, nothing that would provide a clue.

Being gone for days at a time when he was still working certainly provided her with lots of time to cat around, yet he'd never suspected anything. Perhaps she'd found someone else. Will couldn't find it within him to be jealous either. He was just drained of all emotions. He'd been hurt badly and knew it would take time to recover.

Somewhere in North Carolina, he picked up a woman hitch-hiking. She wasn't bad-looking. It was difficult to judge her age. She finally confessed to thirty-six and Will mentally added five years. She had her hair pulled back into a pony tail. She wore cut-off jeans, a polo shirt, and sneakers. Her only baggage was her backpack. She told him her name was Jean, and she was on her way to stay with her cousin in Tampa. She'd been married twice and was running away from an ex-boyfriend who liked to knock her around.

He remembered stopping for pizza and a few beers. They had a few laughs, compared hard times, smoked a joint she had, and found a cheap motel. Suddenly he wasn't feeling so sorry for himself.

Early the next morning Will learned what many unwary men learn about picking up strange women—his wallet was empty and his truck was gone, along with his suitcase, still in the truck. He didn't even have a toothbrush. Looking into the cracked bathroom mirror, Will saw a stranger who needed a shave. He let out a hysterical laugh that he couldn't control. Life had delivered another low blow. He hoped as momentary revenge that the truck's transmission would fail.

With only pocket change, he found himself sticking out his thumb, hoping for a ride south. It was the first day of being truly homeless, though he'd been heading in that downhill direction.

Now, Altoona, Pennsylvania, was a long way away, and it was someplace he hoped he'd never see again, even in his dreams. It took him a week to walk and hitch short rides in order to reach southern Georgia. A week's worth of whiskers added to his wild and unruly look. Drivers were being cautious and passed him by. He'd heard that Georgia state police were not kind to vagrants and gypsies, so he stayed on secondary roads, walking with his head down. He'd lost track of time and didn't know which day it was, but he did know that he was still heading south using the morning sun as his compass.

Luck turned his way when he found an isolated trailer hidden in a clump of Live Oak trees down a long dirt road. The first thing he noticed was no mailbox beside the road. Will proceeded carefully, not seeing any vehicles or dogs to raise an alarm. It was a small, singlewide trailer with a canvas awning by the back door and a webbed folding chair that needed attention. Will sat in the shade of the awning and pondered his next move. Sitting and resting felt good! He wasn't sure what he'd do if someone arrived. Probably run.

Hunger made him decide to find food. With a little effort, he forced the cheap door open. It had just one lock that quickly sprung when Will inserted a stick between the jamb and the handle. Now he was a felon for breaking and entering.

After a week of meager scraps, he no longer cared about breaking the law. A few hot meals behind bars didn't seem to be a bad alternative to his present state.

He found a can of beans and ate them cold along with some stale crackers. And he drank some bottled water. In a closet, he found a real treasure trove. There was a one-man mountain tent in shades of tan, green, & brown, a sleeping bag, and a backpack. In the bedroom he discovered a large hunting knife in a leather sheath under the bed. He found a pair of clean jeans that fit reasonably well, a flannel shirt, and a nice pair of hiking boots that fit once he stuffed paper in the toes. In the bathroom, he was able to wash up and trim his beard.

Will debated on spending the night. If this was a weekend retreat, he might be able to spend a few days before leaving. However, he had no idea what day it was. On the other hand, his luck, until now, hadn't been very good, so he opted to leave rather than stay. He took the underwear and socks he found in a dresser drawer and another can of beans from the small pantry. He wanted to travel as light as possible. He left unnoticed.

Later that afternoon Will walked into a small crossroads diner. He told the cook he had no money, but he was hungry and willing to wash dishes. He was rewarded with a hot roast beef sandwich, mashed potatoes with gravy, and two cups of coffee: the best he could remember. He washed dishes, mopped the floor, and cleaned the toilets. As he was leaving, the cook gave him a wrapped sandwich to take with him and wished him good luck. The experience would stay with him for a long time.

His cleaned-up appearance had made the difference.

Because he no longer looked like a vagrant, he got a few more rides. He looked like a hiker headed toward Florida and warmer weather. He loved the sight of palm trees and the smell of ocean air.

As he walked, he kept trying to remember the words to the song John Harper wrote: *Gentle on My Mind*. He wondered if he'd ever meet someone he could truly care about.

He'd lost some weight and felt better than he had in years. He attributed this to all the exercise he was getting by walking miles on end and eating a lot less. Also lots of sun and fresh air helped. So far, he'd survived the harshness of life and experienced a few kindnesses along the way.

While walking, he had loads of time to think and reflect back to better times. Now he could appreciate all the small things he'd taken for granted, like wearing clean clothes and having a hot meal prepared for him when he arrived home. Also, there was the comfortable bed to sleep in every night. And hot showers. That simple, normal life was no longer his and he truly missed it.

Another homeless man guided him to a shelter where he could take a shower, get a hot meal, and have a bed for the night. While there, he listened carefully to the others and learned about good places to stop and places to avoid, like Tampa, where hundreds of homeless people were being pushed from one place to another. Apparently it was already too crowded and the sympathy toward the homeless had turned sour. Will had to find someplace less congested, where he could feel reasonably safe, find a job, and blend-in with the community. It bothered him that he had to steal occasionally just to survive. He decided that if he ever had a steady job again, he'd be more charitable toward those who were in need. He would have truly walked a mile or more in another person's shoes.

Just south of Melbourne, Will discovered a section of Highway One that ran alongside the Indian River. His camouflaged tent was hidden from the highway, just a few feet from the water and adjacent to a small parking area. Several piers had suffered hurricane damage and he could see the remnants from his small sheltered area. He could sit for hours on end and watch sailboats, motor boats, and kayaks pass by. Sometimes he'd wave to them. Pelicans flew overhead and fished close by, ignoring him. After a few days, Will could recognize different pelicans and see the same one sitting on the vertical posts sticking out of the water that was once a pier. They took a proprietary attitude about those posts, he noted.

Will had been in this location a week when one evening he heard a car pull into the parking area. That really wasn't unusual, but what he overheard was.

"Why are we stopping here?" a woman's voice asked. A few moments later, "Stop it! You're tearing my blouse! I said stop it!"

Will could tell by the panic in the woman's voice that she was being molested. He crawled to the edge of the parking area where he had a view of the automobile and could see a silhouette of the occupants. The woman was crying, "Leave me alone and get off me!"

Will walked deftly behind the vehicle, coming around to the driver's side. The windows were down. The man had the woman pushed against the passenger door holding her secure.

"I think the lady wants you to leave her alone," Will said, leaning into the open window and grabbing the man's exposed arm.

"What? Who the hell are you?"

"Let her go now!" Will yelled, surprising himself.

As the man turned toward Will, the woman shot out of the passenger side. "Oh, thank you," she whimpered. "He was trying to rape me."

The man tried to open his door, but Will pushed against it hard enough to contain him. "If I were you, I'd get lost before the law arrives. If you get out, I'll make sure they find you on the pavement here, in a world of hurt. Your choice, dipwad."

With that, the man turned the key in his ignition, backed up, and drove away quickly, forgetting to turn on his lights. Pulling out onto Highway One, he almost hit a passing truck that honked at him.

"Thank you again. I'm grateful that you came by. I don't see your car."

"That's because I don't have one. Are you alright?" In the darkness he could make out that she was trying to hold her torn blouse together.

"I don't know, I guess I'm just scared. We were on a first date and he took me out to dinner. We were on our way back when he suddenly pulled into this place. I thought maybe he had to use the facilities or something."

"So you know who he is?"

Tomorrow is Just Another Road

"I guess so. We met through a dating service. He said his name was Jacob Ashley. I don't know if that's his real name or not."

"Do you have a cell phone with you? You should report this attack to the police."

"Yes, it's here in my purse, but I don't think I'll report it. Look at me, I'm a mess. If it weren't for you, he'd have raped me."

"Can you call someone to come and get you? I'll be happy to stay with you until they arrive. There's a park bench under those trees."

"Where do you live?" the woman asked.

"Believe it or not, I live right here, down by the water, in a tent. I heard you yelling and came up to see what was going on."

"So you're one of those homeless people?"

"Yes I am, but at your service."

"Aren't you nice! Thank God there are still some decent people in this world."

While they waited, sitting at a picnic table, she told Will her name was Emily. She held a part-time job working at a church-sponsored thrift shop in Sebastian. She gave Will directions on how to find it.

"Stop by and I'll see what I can do to get you some decent clothes. What size do you wear?"

"I'm not sure anymore. I've lost some weight. Wait until I show up and you can help me decide. I'm not fussy about clothes."

Two days later, an older model Honda pulled into the parking area. A woman got out and walked over to one of the picnic tables. It was mid-day. She called out, "Hey, Will, are you there?"

At first he didn't recognize her, but she remembered his name and she'd brought a picnic lunch.

"Sorry, I wasn't expecting any company. How are you doing, Emily?"

"I'm better. I notified the dating service and reported him. I was thinking about telling the police but decided they'd ask a lot of questions and want to know where it took place and how you came to my rescue. I thought that might reveal your hiding place and maybe make things difficult for you."

"Thank you, that was very thoughtful. I'm not used to people doing me favors, and I appreciate it."

They ate the sandwiches she'd prepared and talked about their respective lives. Will learned that Emily was thirty-one and lived alone in a trailer park in Sebastian. She'd never been married. She was from Houston and came to Florida to be with her mother who was dying of cancer. After her mother died, she remained in her trailer, slowly eliminating the clutter and giving things to the church thrift shop where she currently worked part-time.

"Think you'll ever go back to Houston?" Will asked.

"I don't know. I like it here and I've made a few friends. The future seems so uncertain and I'm a little confused about what to do next. My recent dating experience has sort of turned me against internet dating services."

Will liked her open way of talking about herself. He wished his circumstances were different so he could ask her out on a date, show her that all men weren't monsters. He'd already shared his story of misadventures.

"If my situation were different Emily, I'd ask you out in a heartbeat. You're a kind, smart, and attractive woman." Romance hadn't been part of his thoughts for quite a while. "If I could find a part-time job, would you be interested in having dinner with me sometime?"

"Yes, I'd like that, Will. In fact, I have an idea. The Loyal Order of Moose has a club not too far from here. I have a friend who tends bar there on weekends. She might be able to find something for you in the kitchen. Would you be interested?"

"Sure, but your friend might be put off by my shaggy appearance."

"I'll tell you what, I'll check with my friend, and later I'll stop back by and give you a haircut."

That day was a new beginning for Will. He recognized that Emily was a giving and warm person, unlike his wife. After cutting his hair, they drove back to her place where she made a simple meal. He thought it was delicious.

Two months later, Will and Emily were living together in the trailer park. Will was working part-time at the Moose Club and volunteering at the thrift store where Emily worked. Emily was constantly hearing kind words about her new boyfriend.

"How did the two of you meet?" was a frequent question to Emily.

"Believe it or not, we met at a park not too far from here," was all the information she cared to share. She no longer worried about the future. She was with a man she cared about, and she knew he felt the same way about her. That was all that mattered. Will taught her that all the material things in life were temporary. He'd learned that the hard way.

Trusting others still took time for Will. He trusted Emily, but he was still a bit distant with her friends and the patrons at the Moose Club. He liked working in the kitchen and cleaning up after the club closed.

One night, after closing, Rod, the manager, was counting the money from the cash register when the back door opened and two masked men entered with pistols. Their faces were partially hidden with red bandanas pulled up over their noses. Will could tell they were Hispanic. One indicated that he should turn around and face the kitchen wall.

"You say no-thing," he whispered in a strong accent. Will studied the man's flannel shirt with the sleeves cut off, revealing a tattoo of a snake coiled around the man's muscular left arm. It looked vaguely familiar.

The other armed man went into the bar area, forcing Rod to lie on the floor. They took all the money and fled out the back door. Seconds later, Will heard an engine start and roar off into the night.

"How much did they get?" Will asked Rod, after locking the back door. He'd left the back door unlocked and open because he still had trash to take out to the dumpster behind the club.

"About four hundred and change."

When the police arrived, Will heard Rod tell them the robbers had taken "thirteen hundred and change." He wondered about that discrepancy. Later, after the police left, Rod explained that he'd already counted out and put away $900 the thieves didn't get. "I'll give you two-fifty, just keep your mouth shut," Rod said.

"That's okay. I don't want it." If he took the hush money, that would make him party to the crime. It also made him wonder about Rod's true character. Was he skimming the club? Probably. Will decided not to make any of this his problem. He'd keep quiet, do his job, and be thankful for the work. And, he'd never trust Rod with any secrets or confide in him in any way.

A week later, Will was at the thrift store, working in the back stacking boxes, when he heard a distinct voice out front.

"You done know no-thing about quality. Dis is cheap leather. I know 'bout dees thinks." The Hispanic man was holding up a pair of used cowboy boots and showing them to another man standing close by. The man holding the boots was wearing a Polo shirt and his arms had the same snake tattoo. Will watched from the storage room door. When nobody was watching, he walked outside and stood in the shade of a palm tree, waiting to see which car the men were driving so he could record the license plate number. These were dangerous men and he had to be careful not to be seen and recognized. They deserved to be caught, however Will didn't want to be involved.

Will noted the faded maroon Toyota Corolla and the license number.

"Be very careful around those two," he warned Emily who was working in the front of the store and noticed Will's strange actions. He told her they were the same men who'd robbed the club the previous week.

"Are you planning to tell the police?" she asked.

"I'm thinking about it."

That evening Will mentioned what he'd seen earlier that day to Rod. "I have the license plate number and description of the car, in case you want to pass it on to the police."

"Listen, Will, I know you think that's the right thing to do, but it isn't. How can I report this information a week later? They'd ask me why I didn't give it to them earlier."

"Just say you happened to recognize them when you saw them leaving the thrift store today. Mention the tattoo."

"I don't think that's enough to go on. Better to drop it. Nobody got hurt. I say forget about it."

Will couldn't forget about it. It bothered him that Rod was so reluctant to do anything. He'd seen the same tattoo. Whatever the reason, Will felt strongly that he had to stay out of it, but not because Rod had told him. Keeping his nose out of other peoples' problems was his nature, and now he had this conflict to wrestle with. He was fortunate not to still be homeless. He had someone to share life's simple pleasures with. He'd walked the life of a homeless person and now appreciated the small gifts every day presented. He knew that life was a fragile commodity. So were peace and love. The scales tipped back and forth for everyone and Will didn't want to cause those scales to tip back to his former way of life.

To get involved could jeopardize his present situation. There was so much riding on his decision. He knew Emily would stand by him regardless, but he wanted her to respect him, to know that he was basically an honest person she could trust.

"What do you think I should do, Emily?"

"Will, I can see this eating at you. Please know that whatever you decide to do, I'll go along with it. I don't want to influence your decision."

That evening he wrote an anonymous note to the police department:

Two Hispanic men robbed The Moose Club last week. Both wore bandanas as masks and were seen leaving by the back door. They were driving a faded maroon Toyota Corolla, license # 768-OHT. The driver had a tattoo of a snake circling his left arm. I hope you catch them.

Eventually the police would question Rod again. Perhaps ask him to identify the suspects. When that happened, Rod would know Will had said something. And, if the suspects weren't held, Will's safety, and that of Emily, would be in jeopardy.

Will's concern soon became a reality. He was sitting on the back steps of Emily's place enjoying a second cup of coffee when a police cruiser pulled into the parking area. Will recognized the deputy; he was the same officer who'd rousted him several times when he was living in a tent by the river. His name tag read Williams.

"Good morning," Will said, trying to hide the worry that was growing inside. Emily was working at the thrift store. He was due there in an hour.

"Yeah, it is. I got a message for you from your former employer. Notice I said former, because you no longer have a job at the club. Rod asked me to tell you not to bother coming in. He also sent over your pay, which I notice isn't much. I took out twenty for my delivery services."

"I guess Rod didn't want to tell me that to my face."

"That's not it. Ya see, Rod and I go back a long way. I stop in now and then for a drink and we were discussing the recent robbery...."

"So you're the officer doing the investigating?"

"Not exactly, however a crime was committed, and any police officer with any information about that crime is empowered to uphold the law and to help catch the criminal element, if you get my drift. Rod hinted that maybe you knew these guys. Maybe from your former life pounding the road and sleeping in a tent."

"No, I don't know them. I never set eyes on either one of them until the night they came in the back door."

"Oh yeah, the *unlocked* back door. Sort of convenient, wouldn't you say?"

"I was mopping the floor and there was still some trash to take out to the dumpster."

"Uh huh. Well, let me tell you something. Washing dishes, mopping floors, and cleaning the crapper doesn't buy you respectability. Rod gave you the job as a favor to a friend. I told him I knew you from kicking you out of the park a couple times. You were a vagrant then and, as far as I'm concerned, you're still a vagrant. You got this temporary address because you're shacked up with some little gal you met at the park. She must be pretty hard up to hook up with you. She could do a lot better."

"What's that supposed to mean?"

"It means I could show her a good time in ways you can't."

"This is beginning to sound like a conflict of interest. I think I'll call the sheriff and ask if you're assigned to investigate the robbery. Somehow I don't think you are. You want to run me off to eliminate some competition, isn't that more like it?"

"Still got that smart mouth, ain'tcha? Get in the cruiser. The back seat, we're going for a ride."

"I need to leave a note for Emily first."

"No, you don't need to leave no note. We're going to check out a few suspects, see if you recognize these guys."

Will had a feeling there was a bit more going on. It was with a great deal of trepidation that he got into the cruiser. Rod must have been worried to have sent this deputy over to bust his chops. They arrived at a small Hispanic community near the railroad tracks. Rod drove up a dirt path slowly. Several men were sitting outside. They stared and nodded as the cruiser crept slowly down the makeshift road. A few chickens scattered.

"Recognize anyone?"

"Nope."

"Well maybe they're living in Fort Pierce." The deputy pulled out onto 66th Avenue and headed south, away from Sebastian.

"So where are we going now? I want to return home."

"I'm not sure where your *home* is right now. All I know is you're out of work and staying with someone temporarily. I might be doing her a favor by getting you out of Dodge."

"You can't do that! All my stuff is back there."

"We'll see what I can do. While I can't prove you were an accomplice to the robbery, you're still a suspect, which is why you no longer work at the club. Rod can't trust you. And I don't like you. So, the best answer to both situations is to put you someplace far away, never to return."

Will knew he was better off not threatening the officer. He had to wait for an opportunity and stay alert. He noticed the police radio wasn't turned on; he hadn't heard any dispatcher calls. That suggested the officer was off-duty and acting on his own.

"Just drop me in Vero Beach. I can find a job there," Will said.

"That's a little too close to what you call home. I was thinking more like the swamp area in the middle of the state. You know, where the alligators are hungry and people don't stop to pick up strangers."

"This is kidnapping you know."

"You got a funny way of interpreting things. Without a hat the sun can do a real number on you out there, particularly if your leg is broken and you can't walk. Sometimes life can be really cruel."

They'd been driving for a good twenty minutes and Will had to do something before they got past civilization, which they'd be approaching soon. Since he wasn't handcuffed, Will lay down on the rear seat and began kicking at the side window.

"Stop that!" The deputy yelled. He pulled off the road and turned around to look at Will. "If you don't stop that kicking, I'll have to shoot you and drop you out there."

Will continued to kick. "Go ahead and shoot. Be sure you don't miss." Cars and trucks were passing close by. Finally the window broke out of the frame. Will reached out and opened the door; he ran across the busy road, almost getting hit by a passing truck that blew its horn.

Hiding behind a row of tall bushes, Will watched the cruiser attempt a U-turn. It took a while before the traffic eased. Will noticed the flashing lights were now on. The deputy drove slowly down the road looking for Will who remained stationed in his temporary hiding place. The deputy would be expecting him to be running instead of remaining close by. Will waited a good hour. In that time, the deputy had traversed the area several times with his lights still flashing.

Finally he gave up. Will started walking along parallel streets going east toward Vero Beach. He had to stay off the main highway as much as possible.

It was afternoon by the time he reached Vero Beach. He found the railroad tracks and walked beside them heading back to Sebastian. It was a good twenty mile hike, with several freight trains passing close by. He knew the deputy would no doubt keep watch of Emily's place. Therefore he'd wait until it was dark before approaching.

From a distance, he saw a police cruiser parked at Emily's. Deputy Williams had the window down and was talking to Emily, all the while smoking a cigarette. Emily had her arms folded across her chest and stood on the top step. Her body language told Will she was being defensive. With the deputy parked in front, Will circled around to enter by the back door. He could hear them talking.

"Someone reported seeing him hitch-hiking on Route Sixty, heading west. I doubt you'll be seeing him anytime soon."

"That's just not like Will to leave without a note or something."

"Yeah, well with vagrants, they only stay in one place for a little while. Then they move on, just like gypsies."

"But he didn't take any of his things. They're still here."

"Maybe he was scared since he's a suspect in that robbery at the club."

"You've got to be kidding me! Will didn't have anything to do with that. In fact..." Emily cut short what she was about to say. She didn't trust the deputy and decided not to mention the anonymous note Will sent. She knew Will was concerned. Now she was beginning to understand why.

"Call me if you hear from him."

Emily stepped inside without responding. When she entered the dark living room she heard Will whisper, "Don't turn on the light."

Will told her about his captive trip and the threats that were made.

"I really don't know what his problem is, but I do know that he has a personal dislike toward me and I don't see that going away. It's probably best for me to move on, but I don't want to go without you." His feelings toward Emily grew stronger every day he was with her.

"I was so worried about you when I got home and there wasn't any note or anything. Then that deputy showed up. There's something about him that makes my skin crawl. When he looks at me, I feel like he's undressing me with his eyes."

"He mentioned that he and Rod go way back."

"Well, you don't have a job at the club anymore, so there's not that much to keep you here except me. To be truthful, Will, I sort of like it here. I wish we weren't having this problem. What can we do?"

Will didn't get much sleep. He wrestled with the problem of what he should do all night. Emily tossed and turned, telling him she was having trouble sleeping as well.

The next morning Will made a decision. Emily drove him to the sheriff's office early and they waited in her car for the sheriff to arrive. Will asked to speak with the sheriff soon after he walked in.

"What can I do for you?" the sheriff asked politely.

"Well, I'm wondering if there's some sort of order out for my arrest."

"Not that I'm aware of. Why?"

"I know this is going to sound fishy. It's just my word against your Deputy Williams and there are no witnesses, but please hear me out."

Will described the incident in detail, trying to remember the exact words that were spoken. The sheriff listened without interrupting. Emily confirmed that the deputy was at her home last night looking for Will. Will went on to explain he was the person who'd sent the anonymous note.

"Deputy Williams is a patrol officer. He isn't involved with the robbery investigation. So, if what you tell me is true, he was acting on his own. Perhaps because of his friendship with the bartender. I don't recall you being a suspect, but it is interesting that this different scenario has emerged, suggesting that you were somehow involved."

"There's a little more to it that I should explain. Not all of the money was taken. Rod reported a total much greater than what the thieves got away with. He offered me two hundred and fifty to keep quiet. Maybe he's worried I would say something later."

"Okay, here's what we're going to do. First, I'm going to put you in another office and have you put everything you've told me down on paper. I want you to sign and date it. I'll make sure Deputy Williams stays out on patrol while you're here so he doesn't accidentally see you leaving. His cruiser is in for repairs for a broken window, so that part of your story fits, but he said someone threw a rock.

"I'll have one of my detectives talk with this Rod again. Maybe he'll tell us a different story, maybe not. Either way, I'd appreciate it if you'd keep an extra-low profile for a few days. Call me if Deputy Williams shows up at your place again."

Will wasn't sure if the sheriff believed him, but he felt better telling him everything. He had to remain hidden for a while, but that was the easy part. He'd remain inside Emily's place and not answer the phone or the door.

The next afternoon, Emily was working at the thrift store and Will was taking a nap when he heard some noise at the kitchen door. Someone had tried the handle and found the door locked. Now there was a scratching sound. Suddenly the door was open and Will heard footsteps. Will picked up the phone and dialed 911 just in time to see Deputy Williams walk into the room.

"Put down the phone. I had a feeling you'd turn up here. Let's take another little ride. This time I'm going to handcuff you since you're now a fugitive."

"What is the nature of your emergency?" An operator asked. Will had put down the phone but hadn't disconnected the call.

"It's alright, I'm handling it," the deputy responded, hanging up the phone. "Thought you had me out-smarted, didn't you?"

"Doesn't matter, at least they know you're here. Last time I checked, I wasn't a fugitive, so maybe you're chasing the wrong person, Deputy."

"I don't think so. And in case you're wondering, I've got some friends who told me about your recent visit to see the sheriff. He won't believe anything you told him about me. It will be my word against, let's see...somebody who didn't bother to stick around. Let's go."

"You're making a terrible mistake. I have no idea why you've picked me to be so hateful toward."

"I'll tell you why. You're a piece of garbage. You were hanging around, living in a filthy tent down by the water, bothering people. We don't need the likes of you around here. I've told you that before and you didn't listen. So I'm through talking." The deputy pushed Will into the back seat and slammed the door. "If you kick the door, I'll break both your legs!"

Kicking the doors or the windows wouldn't work since Will was wearing only his socks.

"This is a false arrest and you know it. In fact, it could be kidnapping since there isn't any warrant out for my arrest. You're keeping me against my will!" Will yelled.

"Shut your pie hole. I'm gonna finish what I started, only this time I'll have more satisfaction."

"How much did Rod pay you to do this?"

"Me and Rod are buddies. He didn't have to pay me anything."

"Too bad, he offered me two-fifty to keep my mouth shut. You should hold him up for at least five hundred."

"See, that just goes to prove how stupid you are. Why didn't you take him up on that offer?"

"That would have made me part of the robbery."

"Yeah, like you've never taken anything that didn't belong to you."

Will regretted this part of the conversation and decided not to comment. To survive, he had taken things, but he didn't consider himself to be a thief. He wished he could give it all back. They were on 58th Ave., going south, when two cruisers with lights flashing pulled Williams over. The sheriff got out of one of the cruisers.

"I'm just getting this homeless bum out of our jurisdiction, Boss."

"Don't say another word, Deputy. We've got it all recorded."

Will was un-cuffed and switched to another cruiser. Deputy Williams took his place in the back seat with handcuffs. The sheriff explained that the replacement cruiser Deputy

Williams was driving had been wired to record everything said inside the cruiser as well as on the radio. The 911 operator had also reported what she'd heard when Will called. It all supported what Will had volunteered earlier. The plan now was to trap Rod using Williams. If Deputy Williams cooperated, they might give him some consideration.

"I'm a little concerned about retaliation after all this gets sorted out," Will said.

"I can understand that. However, Deputy Williams will get a severe reprimand, and he'll be warned to stay away from you."

A reprimand! That wasn't much punishment, and a warning to stay away. If he was smart, Williams would keep his distance, but Will didn't think he was all *that* smart. Some night in the near future, on some deserted road, Will could almost picture another encounter. That's just the way Williams was wired. For the moment, Will and Emily were safe; they had a little time to plan their next move without rushing. But, it was only a matter of time....

Will was back to thinking in terms of one day at a time. It was going to take some time to build a new life with Emily at his side. He was satisfied that he'd done the right thing. He'd heard about a group in Vero Beach that helped homeless people. Will felt he could be helpful at someplace like that. After all, he'd walked a lot of miles as a homeless person and knew exactly how that felt, never really knowing where the road, and the next day, would take him. ."

Not My First Rodeo

"Hey cowboy, need a ride?" the woman asked, pulling alongside Gabe. She was driving a shiny black Cadillac convertible with the top down.

The driver was a smiling, middle-aged redhead wearing a bright red party dress hiked up high enough to show off good-looking legs, in the center of which was a long neck beer bottle standing upright. It was a scene he'd never expect to see, but it did appear her thighs were the perfect bottle holder. Gabe was momentarily hypnotized, thinking what a great beer commercial this could be. He didn't attempt to hide his grin as he opened the passenger door.

"Sure do," Gabe said. He started to throw his backpack into the back seat, then noticed a man curled up, apparently asleep. "How far are you going?"

"All the way, cowboy. Where you headed?"

"I'm hoping to get to Florida, eventually. No hurry. I'll get there when I get there."

"What's in Florida?" she asked, pulling back onto the highway, slewing some gravel. She turned down the radio which was tuned to a popular Country/Western station.

"Warm weather, sand, palm trees, and the ocean."

Gabe had started walking just before sun up and this would be his second ride. The woman's red party dress was in sharp contrast to the white leather seats. He also noticed she was wearing red high heels: something he didn't expect to see this early in the day, unless she was partying all night.

His mental warning system was flashing a caution. This could be big trouble, and trouble seemed to follow him everywhere he went lately.

"Uh huh. What about those Palmetto bugs and the hurricanes?"

"What about them? Every place has its pluses and minuses. I just think Florida has more pluses." Gabe looked over his shoulder at the other passenger in the back. "That guy back there sleeping?"

"I think he's passed out. He's been that way since I left the party. He was supposed to drive me home. This is his car, or at least I think it is. Check the registration in the glove box. I think he said his name was Howard something or other."

"Where was this party?" Gabe asked, checking the contents of the glove box. "Does the name Howard Osgood ring a bell?"

"Yeah, that's him. Apparently we went to high school together. I don't remember him, but he said he remembers me. Said he once had a crush on me. Actually, I think it was just a pickup line he uses."

"So was this a class reunion?"

"No, I drove up to Chattanooga with a girlfriend. It was supposed to be a big surprise party for some guy's birthday. She said I'd recognize a few old friends and we'd have some fun. She was hoping her ex was going to be there. She was also hoping to get back together with him. I warned her it wasn't a good idea."

"So where's your girlfriend now?"

"Good question. She and her ex left the party together and that's the last I saw of her. She left me stranded there with a bunch of drunks. This is the second time she's done that to me. Howie back there offered to drive me home and never made it past the steering wheel. I poured him in the back seat and he's been like that for the past hour."

"Wouldn't this be a little out of the way for him? I mean, does he know where you live?"

"Honey, very few people know where I actually live. I

usually give them my sister's address. That's where my girlfriend picked me up yesterday."

"Is that where we're headed now, back to your sister's place?"

"Yeah, my car is there. So is the rest of my stuff. I gotta take a shower and change clothes."

"What are we going to do about Howard back there?"

"I'm thinking we leave him and the car somewhere. I'll follow you in my car. It'll be a big surprise for Howie when he wakes up. Be a bitch to explain to his wife if he's married.

"So tell me, do all your ex's live in Texas?" she laughed as she asked. Gabe took the hint that it was a different way of asking if he was married. He glanced at the steering wheel and her left hand--no ring. He was trying to guess her age and put it around fifty, give or take.

"No, my ex is back there in Loudon, just south of Knoxville, living with some jerk who isn't worth the bullet to kill him," he replied.

"Is the old flame still burning?" she inquired.

"No, it's been over between us for a few years now. We disagreed on too many things." While he guessed that her red hair came from a tube, he could tell that she had the temper of a true redhead. She told him that she considered the door closed when it came to her ex.

Gabe hadn't planned on getting into this discussion and wondered how it came up so quickly. He hadn't heard from Mary-Alice in a long time, then one night she had called and left a brief message asking if he'd be in the area anytime soon. It sounded like she might need something. He no longer had feelings for Mary-Alice, and this was the first contact in over four years, but out of curiosity he detoured over to Knoxville on his way south.

When he arrived, he discovered she was living with a full-time drunk. Gabe saw several bags of beer bottles and cans sitting on the porch. She appeared surprised to see him. When he mentioned the phone message, she acted like she didn't know anything about it. There he was, standing on the porch, with her drunken boyfriend yelling in the background. Gabe was pretty sure she was embarrassed by the scene. She didn't appear to be stoned, but maybe she was. It was an awkward moment.

As he was getting back into his truck, he heard the boyfriend yell, "Best you don't come back!"

The next moment he fell to the ground, having been hit by something hard from behind. Gabe instinctively rolled and jumped to his feet just in time to avoid a wicked kick aimed at where his head would have been. The fight was over when Gabe broke the boyfriend's nose. He held back because, with all the adrenaline pumping, it would have been easy to kill the boyfriend with a few more well-placed blows.

As he got into his truck he heard several shots and felt the truck settle as both tires on his side went flat. It was an old truck, not worth another oil change, so he grabbed his backpack and slid out the passenger-side door. Mary-Alice was standing on the porch aiming a rifle at him. He decided it was a fitting ending: to leave the truck where it sat in the driveway, rusting and dying slowly. Mary-Alice could keep it for a new lawn ornament. He threw the keys as far as he could throw them into the brush. He hoped it was full of poison ivy.

Gabe's nature was to walk away from most confrontations unless he was physically threatened. The drunk didn't know how lucky he was to still be breathing air, even through a broken nose.

Gabe had used his cell phone to call 911, reporting that a man was threatening to kill his girlfriend. Shots had been fired. He'd let the deputies take over. Mary-Alice probably wouldn't call him again.

"You want a drink?" asked the red-head, reaching back into a cooler on the rear floor. She held up another long neck beer and managed to twist off the cap and still steer. It was a well-practiced maneuver.

"Thanks, I'll pass. It's a little early for me to start drinking." *Mainly because he hadn't had anything to eat in the last 12 hours,* he thought and then considered about asking if she wanted him to drive while she got some rest.

"But you do drink don't you?"

"Oh yeah, I can put it away, big time, when I'm in the mood. But the mood never hits me until later in the day."

"So what's it take to put you in the mood early?"

"Right now, it wouldn't take much."

"I see you looking at my legs. They're too white, I haven't been out in the sun enough."

"I like the way you keep that bottle from tipping. And you have great legs!"

"For an old broad. That's what you were about to say, wasn't it?"

"I wouldn't call you an old broad. I'd say you're a very attractive woman with a great body, and I don't see a ring on your left hand, either. So what happened with your last boyfriend?"

"I've had so many boyfriends I can't remember half their names anymore. I've been married three times and I'm not interested in doing that again, unless you've got a ton of money and a bad ticker."

They were driving south on Highway 411—it ran parallel to I-75. The route was scenic with mountain ridges to the east. Catching a ride on I-75 was too difficult despite the heavy truck traffic. Nobody wanted to stop when traveling at high speeds. Roads like 411 allowed for a slower pace and more places to stop.

"Well, since you're not in any big hurry to get to Florida, we'll make a quick stop at my sister's house which is in Jasper. You ever heard of Jasper?" Before he could answer, she added, "Didn't think so. I need to check my mail and get some of my stuff there. Then we'll stop off at my place before we head on down to sunny Florida. I wasn't planning on taking a vacation, but what the heck, why not? Life is too short to waste it waiting around for something interesting to happen, right? Let me tell you something, cowboy: absolutely nothing interesting happens in Jasper either. Even the grass takes its good old time growing."

"How far away is it to your place from Jasper?"

"Oh, about ten miles. It's just a little jerk-water town, smaller than Jasper, so you never heard of it. Nobody has. I grew up there and moved away as soon as I learned about the birds and the bees, know what I'm saying?"

"I think so. You got introduced to sex at an early age."

"Thirteen and my mother didn't do a thing about it."

"Did she know?"

"Of course she knew. She didn't care. She had five other kids to look after. I'm the oldest."

"So you left home and went where?"

"I ran off and stayed with my aunt in Nashville. She was a school teacher and a strict one. If it hadn't been for her, I would have dropped out of school."

"And now you're back there?"

"I'm the only one who cares about the place. My folks are dead, my brothers and sisters have no interest, and it's not something that's worth a whole lot. It's just me and a lifetime of old memories."

"Sounds to me like a good place to hide."

"Oh, you're good! How'd you pick up on that?"

"Just a hunch. You left at an early age, getting cheated out of some childhood years. What's there to go back for unless it's a temporary retreat? Someplace nobody would ever think of looking. Maybe not even know about." It sounded like the kind of place he was looking for.

"Thank you, Doctor Phil. Want to analyze my sex life while you're at it?"

"That might be a little too complicated, given what you've mentioned so far. Hell, you don't even know my name, and I don't know yours."

"Good, let's keep it like that. Strangers can talk to one another more truthfully than friends or relatives. For now you can call me Cathy."

Gabe thought about that for a moment and had to agree; there was some truth in that logic. This woman was a mystery yet interesting at the same time. She fit his idea of what some people called cougars—older women who hit on younger studs for one-night stands. There was more to her story and he felt sure it would all come out eventually, when she was ready to tell it. Meanwhile, he had to be careful not to fall into a trap of revealing too much about himself.

"So tell me about your love life. I'll bet you've had a lot of women."

"Let me put it this way, if we wind up in the sack together, rest assured, it won't be my first rodeo."

"No, and it won't be your last either. I can tell that much talking with you. What kind of work do you do?"

"You name it, I've done it. Mostly I pick up jobs in construction." He used that as a convenient cover story whenever the question surfaced.

"Good way to keep in shape. It explains your tan."

"Yeah. I've been bouncing around for quite a while. It's time I looked for something permanent."

"I don't know, I think you still have a little wild left in you. I hope I'm right."

"I think there's still a lot of wild left in you, too."

"Well, last night was supposed to be wild, but it won't measure up to tonight. I've got a feeling it's gonna be a long one."

"Maybe you better rest up then and let me drive for a while." It appeared he had a ride all the way to Florida. The big question was, did he want it. The price just might be more than he was willing to pay. That was happening a lot lately. And Howie, in the back seat, was about to learn that lesson.

Another Road

The quest for privacy and freedom carries a high price, something homeless people seek, yet can't afford. They move from place to place, like gypsies and vagrants...because they are an embarrassment to those more fortunate.

"You can't sleep in the park!" the deputy yelled.

Deputy LaMarr Puckett hated homeless people. While it was his job to enforce the law, sometimes his anger surfaced at moments like this and it was difficult to control. He kicked the man still in the sleeping bag.

The park was more like a large roadside rest area with a magnificent view of the Indian River. The sparse remains of vertical supports sticking out of the water suggested a pier had been there. It was a visual reminder of the last major hurricane to pass through the area. Several large palm trees had been uprooted and left to rot. Decay was also apparent in the adjacent vacant lots along Highway One, reminding visitors that even paradise took a hit now and then.

"Why don't you just arrest me, then I'll have a better place to sleep tonight?" the homeless man said, all the while grinning at the officer. He smelled of week-old body odors. His hair and whiskers made him look wild, but his sparkling blue eyes and sense of humor hinted this was an intelligent human being down on his luck, trying to survive against the elements and the prejudices of his fellow man. At the moment, Deputy LaMarr Puckett was about to reinforce that prejudice.

"Oh no, get your shit picked up and move along. I don't want to see you anywhere near here again, understand?"

The deputy stood three inches shorter than the homeless man and carried at least forty more pounds. His baton and pistol easily made up for the difference in height. In addition, the deputy's mean streak was enough to make most people wary. In contrast, the homeless man had a passive disposition, not wanting to hurt anyone or anything, including animals. What he wanted most was just to be left alone. He lived every day in search of peace and quiet, and this area appealed to him more than any other place he'd been.

"Well, since you put it to me so nicely, how can I refuse?"

"Don't give me any lip or I'll put a hurt on you that you'll be a long time remembering." LaMarr disliked anyone who questioned his authority. In addition to homeless people, he disliked the gypsy-types that occasionally passed through River View. And he hated young kids who showed no respect for the law. He also hated bikers who refused to pull over because they could out-run his aging police cruiser.

"They used to call that police brutality. I guess you don't have any compassion for your brothers less fortunate than you."

The homeless man was bent over, gathering his few belongings into a worn, surplus canvas duffle bag he'd found in a nearby dumpster. It was more convenient than pushing a shopping cart to haul his stuff; the duffle bag gave him more flexibility. It also took him back to another time when he shouldered a similar bag in the military. He wasn't afraid of the deputy—he just didn't like to engage in confrontations. He'd seen more than his share in another life.

"Get this straight, shithead. You ain't my brother in any shape or manner. If I haul your ass in, you'll be picking up litter alongside this here highway for a week. Some of it's probably yours."

"No sir, I don't litter. I use one of the trash barrels the town has so conveniently put everywhere." Actually, picking up trash had some appeal in that it also promised a few free meals and a safe place to sleep, provided he didn't have to do it with cracked ribs or a knot on his head, both of which he felt sure the deputy would be happy to provide. He had to keep his distance and use the duffle bag as a shield if the deputy came at him with his baton. He hated to scuffle with anyone, but particularly with a police officer. It was always better to just walk away, something he was used to doing.

The deputy didn't see the humor in this remark, even though there wasn't a trash receptacle anywhere in sight. He knew there should have been at least two and couldn't remember the last time he saw any. A green port-o-potty was the only convenience in the small park, along with a few picnic tables and a blackened stationary grill. Travelers passing through the small town of River View frequently stopped at the roadside park to marvel at the million-dollar view of the adjacent river and small islands beyond. One of the islands was a bird sanctuary.

River View was just a speck on most Florida maps with a total population of 2700 people, give or take. The population rose slightly during the winter months when Snow Birds migrated south for the warmer weather. Most continued on to places like Vero Beach, Stuart, or Jupiter. Snow Birds also accounted for the majority of the traffic violations LaMarr wrote. One reason was the speed limits varied from one short section to another along this stretch of Highway One.

The shabby roadside park was a convenient place to catch speeders going north or south. LaMarr took particular delight in picking up young female hitchhikers, enjoying whatever they offered in order to not be arrested. Chasing out homeless bums, so he could have the park to himself, was another necessary item on his list of things that needed to be done regularly.

Haskell Ledbetter seldom revealed his real name for obvious reasons. He hated his parents for ever giving him a name like Haskell, even though it had been his great-grandfather's name. Instead, he told people his name was Henry. Therefore, most of his life had been a lie. He ran away from home when he was fifteen, joined the Marines when he was seventeen, and lied about his age and where he was from. He'd lied about his age enough that he no longer remembered his exact age and didn't care. He became a loner at an early age and liked it that way.

He'd survived as a POW in Nam when many others didn't. The secret, he'd learned and practiced, was to hide in a mental zone where nobody could reach him. It was a peaceful place, and it gave him solitude. Later, after the war ended, he found it difficult to adjust to civilian life, refusing to obey authorities of any stripe. He refused to get a driver's license and he refused to pay taxes, resulting in a court-ordered stay at the iron bar Hilton. He even refused medical attention at the VA hospital because he knew deep down he wasn't crazy. And, he disliked little men with just enough authority to make life miserable for others. Deputy LaMarr Puckett was a perfect example.

It was easy to dislike the deputy for rousting him from his sleeping arrangement at River View Park. Henry had hidden on several occasions when the deputy was parked there. He'd watched LaMarr enjoying a sexual moment with some young truant passing through the area. The deputy seemed to have a schedule for arriving mid-afternoon and leaving close to 5:00. Today was an exception, and he'd caught Henry by surprise, kicking his sleeping bag and waking him in the early hours of the day.

"If I were you, I'd keep moving south and make sure you're out of my jurisdiction," LaMarr snarled. He was having trouble containing his temper.

"And just how far south would that be, sir?"

"Oh you're a real smart mouth, aint-cha?" LaMarr pulled out his baton, which he usually left in his cruiser, and held it ready to swing at the defenseless man gathering up his belongings.

At that precise moment a truck's horn blew behind them.

"Hey buddy, what d'ya think you're doing? Put down that club and try me on for size," the truck driver yelled.

Henry took advantage of the momentary distraction, picked up his bundle and hurried away. A few minutes later, the same truck pulled up beside him and the driver offered him a lift south.

"Thanks for that interruption. That guy has a bad attitude," Henry said. He was grateful for the ride.

"I'd say it goes beyond that. Someday somebody will tear him a new one."

Henry wasn't afraid of the police officer, he just didn't like confrontations or violence. He'd already seen more than most men.

"You want something to eat?" the truck driver asked a few minutes later. He pulled into a 7-Eleven.

Henry gratefully accepted a hotdog and a soda. Then, reaching into his pants pocket, he pulled out two wrinkled dollar bills and bought two lottery tickets. It was an impulsive act but he suddenly felt lucky. He'd avoided a beating and had gotten a lift as well as something to eat. He was on a roll. Before leaving, Henry took advantage of the toilet facilities. On his way back to the truck, he noticed the clerk looking out the front window; he didn't see Henry sneak two Almond Joys into a pocket.

"So, what do you plan to do if you win the lottery?" the truck driver asked.

"To tell you the truth," something he seldom did, "I haven't given it much thought. Maybe buy a small farm and plant some vegetables. That'd be fun," Henry said.

"Well, I wish you luck," the driver said, letting Henry out at a convenient spot, a block away from another park. This park was larger, in the middle of Sebastian, but it didn't afford any privacy. Henry decided he liked his old park better and would probably venture back after dark. He sat on top of a covered picnic table and watched the foot traffic pass by. It was way too busy here. Music was playing from somewhere close by and he noticed a lot of biker activity. He smiled, thinking about all those bikers roaring by River View, driving the deputy crazy. The man was borderline already, he decided. Probably wouldn't take much to push him over the edge.

The truck driver's interruption put LaMarr into a near rage. As a result, he ticketed several motorists who were barely exceeding the speed limit. He had trouble writing the tickets because his hand shook. To calm down, he drove to a local gas station and convenience store that served coffee. LaMarr helped himself to a large cup with extra cream and sugar, grabbed a frosted doughnut, and walked past the clerk without paying or saying thank you. After all, his presence there probably prevented a robbery. That was his rationalization.

Sitting in the patrol car with his still-hot coffee at River View Park, LaMarr let his thoughts drift to Cindy. He wondered what she might be doing now.

Cindy was LaMarr's girlfriend. He lived with her in a single-wide mobile home in Indio Estates, a mobile home park two miles inland from the water where lot rents were much less expensive. Cindy's ex-husband still owned the trailer and allowed her to live there with their two teen-aged sons in lieu of alimony and support. Cindy allowed LaMarr to live there, provided he paid the utilities and bought the groceries. It was supposed to be a win-win situation for both of them. Until lately.

Cindy worked part-time at the local VFW hall as a barmaid. LaMarr noticed the manager, Earl Peabody, was taking an increased interest in her and her still-shapely body. Even with a few extra pounds, she still had a cute ass and boobs the guys at the hall liked to oogle.

LaMarr suspected Cindy's amorous feelings toward him were both false and diminishing, not that it was ever more than an indulgence. He figured it was just a matter of time and she'd cut him loose. But for now he guessed that she liked the added financial support he provided.

He'd always known their relationship wouldn't be long term. What she needed, and wanted, was a sugar daddy—he'd do for now, but he knew that it wasn't forever.

Her boss, Earl, didn't fit that picture very well, either. LaMarr, being naturally suspicious, frequently stalked Cindy's movements. He knew Cindy's boss was married, where the guy lived, and the kind of truck he drove. Sooner, or later, he felt certain he'd catch Cindy and Earl in a compromising situation. Then both of them would pay dearly for their illicit actions. He didn't love Cindy, just enjoyed her attention, even if it was faked sometimes. He wasn't overly jealous that other men showed an interest in her. After all, it was part of her job to hustle for big tips. Sometimes she had to flirt and wiggle her ass a little, even show some cleavage. But he sure as hell didn't want any of her customers making a move on her.

To be certain, he was often sitting outside, across from the parking lot, with a view of the VFW hall at closing time. He didn't care if Cindy saw him or not.

That night, Henry was back at his favorite park where he'd been rousted. Earlier, he'd come across an old blue plastic tarp that would work as a small tent. He found a secluded spot close to the water that was not visible from the parking lot. He was hidden by a cluster of palm trees, sea grapes, and a bank that sloped down to the water.

The day had provided several good finds in addition to the discarded tarp. Behind a mall he found several lengths of discarded rope. In a dumpster he found two very used, worn out mops. The long shafts were perfect for support poles. And, he found a package of stale cookies which he was shared with his new-found hungry friend.

The dog was part German Shepherd and part Husky, making him look more like a wolf. The dog seemed starved and Henry gave him half the cookies, feeding them slowly. After eating, the dog lay down beside Henry and licked his hand as if to say thank you. Henry patted the dog's head and rubbed his ears whispering softly, "It's you and me against the world, buddy. We gotta look after each other." Henry had no doubt his new friend understood.

Henry promptly named the dog and Wolf slept at Henry's feet, near the open end of the makeshift tent. The next morning another vagrant tried to approach Henry's tent only to be warned off by Wolf's low growl. The man quickly backed away. Henry pet Wolf and whispered to him, thankful to have the dog keeping watch. He doubted that Deputy LaMarr Puckett would ever get another chance to surprise him. Henry was thankful for Wolf's arrival. They were both pitted against a harsh existence, each willing to protect the other. Being able to adapt to awkward situations was Henry's secret for survival. With Wolf by his side, he stood an even better chance.

Another Road

Three days passed before Henry learned that his two-dollar investment had indeed made him a millionaire many times over. The manager of the 7-Eleven was a Pakistani named Haidar. Everyone called him Harry, and he was elated to see Henry and celebrated by giving him a free cup of coffee along with a frosted doughnut. Wolf received a bowl of milk.

Henry knew he'd have difficulty avoiding his newly acquired status. Someone mentioned that it wouldn't be long before the media would want to interview him and learn about his rags-to-riches story. He'd have to invent something that sounded plausible. Meanwhile, he needed a new place to hide.

Harry agreed to lend Henry fifty dollars so he could get a haircut and buy some better clothes at a nearby thrift store. A woman working in the store barely recognized him. She'd given him a few discarded items in the past. Her name was Mildred Glass. Henry knew she was a widow and lived alone, volunteering at the shop three days a week. She'd told him all this on one of his earlier visits.

With his hair cut and whiskers gone, she thought he was a decent-looking man. He seemed polite and didn't look dangerous. In fact, he seemed almost shy.

When she learned of his plight, she offered him a temporary place to stay until he could make other arrangements. The offer wasn't entirely selfless because she had a few things that needed some attention, like a screen door that didn't close properly. She knew she could find a few more projects later. She was also aware that he had some money coming, the sum of which she could not comprehend. Anything over a thousand dollars was a lot of money to Mildred, who relied on her late husband's social security to get by. However, Mildred's generosity toward Henry wasn't motivated by the money he had coming; it was just her nature to be kind to those less fortunate.

Everything seemed to be happening way too fast to suit Henry. He accepted Mildred's kind offer to use her spare bedroom, provided she allowed Wolf to sleep on the porch. Henry never went anywhere now without Wolf by his side or close.

Mildred guessed she was a few years older than Henry. He in turn suspected she was close to sixty. She decided that it was nice having someone to cook for and share a meal with.

Within a few day's time, everyone was commenting on how much younger Mildred appeared. The gray in her hair had suddenly changed to a softer brown and she wore a hint of makeup. She baked Henry an apple pie, which he claimed was the best he'd ever had. It became obvious to all she was happy to have a house guest and tongues began to wag.

Henry remained the perfect gentleman: polite, appreciative of her cooking, complimentary about how she looked, and he never cussed. Mildred never really liked animals, but she quickly warmed to Wolf. It amazed her how the dog would respond to any command Henry gave. Mostly Henry whispered to the dog and the dog seemed to understand, picking up his ears and tilting his head.

After dinner, Henry watched the weather channel. He had no real interest in politics, tax proposals, or candidates running for office. Henry felt that even honest men with honorable intentions could be swayed and influenced. Power and influence soon eroded into corruption, something he hated. In the past he'd read discarded newspapers, usually a few days old, and found very little that interested him. World events didn't influence his day-to-day agenda.

He savored the few hours he had left before things would change.

Mildred drove him to Tallahassee to collect his fortune. Before they left, Henry got a post office box, at Mildred's suggestion, so he'd have an official mailing address. Once at the lottery office he had to have his picture taken and provide his social security number. The thirty-three million he'd won suddenly became less when taxes were deducted. Henry was given a check for $650,000 as the first installment, with a similar amount coming every year for the next twenty-five years. It further annoyed him that he had to open a checking account at a local bank. It was necessary to cash the check. He deposited most of it. Everything he disliked was suddenly being forced upon him. He had no desire to be somebody important, to be in the news, or to be recognized.

Henry knew Mildred's home wasn't sufficient to keep media people from invading his privacy. Once again he felt trapped. Periodically his mind would wander back to another time, when he was a prisoner, confined to a small hole in the ground. Mildred's mobile home park was close enough that Henry was able to walk to his favorite 7-Eleven, where every day he bought a local newspaper. He read all the classified ads, searching for small farms for sale. He then decided that he needed transportation to visit the various locations he wanted to scout.

Without hesitation Harry, his newest best friend, had a cousin who had a used Ford pickup truck he was willing to sell. Henry had no idea what the truck was worth. He bought it without any attempt to haggle over the price. Now Wolf was able to ride in the bed of the truck and Henry was able to move about freely. He still didn't have a driver's license and had to be extra careful. On several occasions he passed Deputy LaMarr Puckett who never recognized him. It took will power to not flip him the bird.

Meanwhile, Mildred had a niece she wanted Henry to meet. Mildred told Henry that while her niece was attractive, there was some baggage; she was divorced with two kids, both teenagers. Mildred was hoping she'd remarry so the kids would have a normal home life. Right now, her niece was living with a cop who was abusive. Mildred feared that soon things might get out of hand. So, if Henry would agree to meet her, and if things worked out between them, maybe life would be more pleasant for all concerned. Henry had his doubts that the boyfriend would agree. Cops were to be avoided at all cost. It was Henry's plan to stay one step ahead of trouble.

"I don't know, Mildred. I'm used to being alone. Me and Wolf get along just fine, and I'm not sure I want a woman in my life, particularly one with kids." *What she probably wants is to find someone to put her kids through college*, Henry thought to himself. This was the beginning. Everyone from here on would be after his money.

"Henry, listen to me. She's a great cook. She's sexy-looking and guys are always giving her the eye, so you can assume she'd be fun to be with if you take my meaning." She actually winked at him, causing him to smile.

"So why hasn't she hooked up with mister right already?"

"I keep asking her the very same question. She says she's happy with things as they are, but I know that's not true."

"Right now, having a woman in my life is not a high priority. And one with kids doesn't get me excited. One who has a cop as a boyfriend certainly puts her off my radar. I'm sorry, Mildred." He didn't want any confrontations with the law.

"Well at least do me a favor and agree to meet her. She's getting off work early today to have dinner with us. It'll just be the three of us. She's dying to meet you, and I know you'll like her."

Once again Henry felt trapped. He liked Mildred and didn't want to hurt the woman's feelings, so he agreed. He explained that after dinner, he had plans to visit a farm he'd seen listed in the newspaper. It was being auctioned by the bank. It seemed to fit what he was looking for.

Cindy arrived a little after six. Henry had to agree the woman looked terrific and smelled very nice. She was blond and very shapely with long legs sticking out of a rather short skirt. Henry wondered if the high heels were for his benefit since most women who worked behind bars wore more sensible shoes.

"I read about your rags-to-riches story in the newspaper and I've wanted to meet you ever since. Aunt Millie told me you were staying with her." Cindy hoped she didn't sound too gushy. For an older guy, he didn't look too bad. She could see he was shy.

"Yes, well she's certainly been a big help when I really needed it." He looked over at Mildred and saw her blushing. "You learn a lot about people through their generosity." It was the most philosophical thing he'd said in years.

"Aunt Millie says you're looking for a small farm. Have you ever farmed?"

"Nope, don't know much about it. But I do know that a farm puts you farther away from your neighbors, and that spells privacy, which is what I'm looking for. Also, it will be a good place for Wolf. He needs some place where he can run." Wolf heard his name mentioned and came over and sat beside Henry, waiting for his ears to be rubbed.

"I think that dog loves you," Cindy said.

"Oh, I know he does. He also knows that I love him, too."

"My kids would love to have a dog, but they won't allow pets where I live."

The suggestion wasn't missed. Henry knew he was being set up. When he said he had a farm he wanted to check out, Cindy asked if she could ride along. Once again, he was trapped but agreed since Cindy knew the whole county well. So did Deputy LaMarr Puckett who was parked a block away so he could watch Mildred's mobile home without being noticed. He knew Cindy was visiting her aunt who was currently living with some guy she met recently. Cindy indicated he was rich. Somehow that didn't compute. If he was rich, why was he living in an older mobile home? Why not buy something nice and new? There were very few rich people living in River View. If you had money, you wanted to be in Vero Beach.

They took Henry's truck. Cindy gave Henry directions on the best way to get to the farm just outside a small rural town called Fellsmere. The farm was west of I-95 by about four miles on a dirt road. Since it hadn't rained in a while, the Ford stirred up a lot of trailing dust. They found the auction sign and turned down a long dirt drive.

A broken split-rail fence ran along one side of the drive with the single story farmhouse sitting back behind a cluster of tall trees. There was a barn beyond the house that appeared to be in decent shape in contrast to the house, which appeared to have been vacant a long time. The roof had missing shingles and the gutters were hanging at an angle. Several windows were broken and the front door was hanging open. The porch had some missing boards.

"You're not seriously interested in buying this old place are you?" Cindy asked.

"Yep. Looks like my kind of place. I've lived in worse. Come on, Wolf, let's explore your new home." Wolf jumped out and ran beside Henry to the barn. The doors were open, revealing an old Ford tractor with its engine exposed. The battery was missing and the tires were almost flat.

Cindy, in high heels, remained in the truck, wishing she'd brought along some sneakers. Her aunt had warned her that Henry could be a bit strange at times. Anyone interested in this out-of-the-way place certainly was different to say the least.

Suddenly Cindy wasn't as interested as she'd been earlier. Maybe her aunt was a better candidate. If that happened, she could get Mildred to cut her in for some of the money. She couldn't see anyone living this far away from civilization.

A quarter of a mile away, parked in a driveway to another farm, LaMarr watched the activity through field glasses. He didn't like the fact that this stranger in the Ford pickup, with his girlfriend, was looking at this particular farm. Yes, it was being auctioned off next week, and yes, he intended to buy it from the bank. LaMarr had already spoken to the bank and had a fair idea of what it would take to buy the place, the place that was once owned by his grandparents. He'd spent his early years on this very farm. And, if the old rumor was true, there was some hidden cash somewhere, still waiting to be found.

LaMarr had made numerous trips out to the farm once it became abandoned. The previous occupants moved away leaving the place in ruins. They hadn't worked the farm and they hadn't made any of the needed improvements.

LaMarr had the plate number of the truck and, as soon as he was back in his cruiser with his laptop, he'd find out more about this stranger who was suddenly invading his life.

In his discussions with the bank, LaMarr had determined that it would take around $150,000 to win the bid. It was a small farm, only seven acres plus the two buildings. He was prepared to go as high as $175,000 but that was his limit.

"Did you have a nice dinner with your Aunt Millie?" LaMarr asked when Cindy arrived home.

"Yeah, it was okay. Did you fix yourself something?"

"No, I picked up a pizza since you didn't leave anything for me to heat up." The boys always found something to microwave. They never ate at the table with LaMarr.

"Sorry. I never know when you'll be home."

"That's right, you don't. Who was the guy at your aunt's place?"

"I'm surprised you don't know. You seem to know everything else. His name is Henry something or other. He rents a room from my aunt."

"Uh huh. They got something going?"

"Somehow I don't think so. He's nice enough, but a little strange." She didn't want to mention anything more and quickly jumped to another topic.

The day of the auction, LaMarr waited to see where the bid was going. Bidding started at $55,000 and quickly jumped to $80,000. Then the stranger, who turned out to be Henry Ledbetter, bid $90,000. LaMarr decided it was time to jump in and bid $95,000. Sweat soaked his shirt. Henry countered with $125,000. LaMarr was rapidly approaching his limit. He wasn't sure he could actually get much more money in a hurry. He'd have to arrange a mortgage of some kind or a short-term loan. His worrying was short-lived when Henry bid $200,000 and it was over.

The three other bidders, along with LaMarr, dropped out. Henry approached the auctioneer and proceeded to write a check for the full amount. Henry certainly didn't need any keys to the place.

Henry walked back to his truck where Wolf was waiting. "This is your new home now, Wolf." The dog wagged his tail understanding.

It was noon and Henry didn't see any reason to waste the day. In anticipation of winning the bid, he brought along some tools so he could get started on the needed repairs. Henry was prepared to go as high as necessary to get the farm. He didn't really care what it cost; he could afford it and the other bidders couldn't. He was also aware that Deputy LaMarr Puckett was scowling at him. Henry wondered if the deputy finally recognized him. Henry had his back to the crowd when he heard LaMarr behind him.

"You look awfully familiar to me. Have we met somewhere before?"

"If we had, I'm sure I'd remember."

"Wait just a cotton-pickin' minute, I remember now. I read about you in the paper. Yeah, you're the rags-to-riches lottery winner. I knew you when you were in rags alright...at the park. Yeah, that's you, only you don't smell as bad as you did."

"And now I'm a taxpayer in the county, where you work. So in a manner of speaking, I guess you're here to protect all my rights and see to it that nobody trespasses on my property." Henry gave him a big smile.

"Still got that smart mouth! You step out of line and I'll have your ass. I'll be watching your every move from now on."

"I hope I can quote that to your boss. If you'll be spending all your time watching my ass, who's going to be writing tickets out there on the highway?"

"Just remember, you've been warned." LaMarr pointed a finger causing Wolf to start a low growl.

"Guess you'll be missing that free sex you're used to getting from the hitchhikers, huh?"

"You watch your mouth, mister!" LaMarr walked away, ignoring the on-lookers who'd overheard the exchange. Wolf was barking, ready to leap, but Henry whispered to him to stay and he did. LaMarr didn't realize how close he'd come to being overtaken by the strong dog.

Henry moved into the barn since the roof was in decent shape, better than the house. The house needed a lot of attention. It would take several months to remodel. Henry opened an account with Lowe's and had materials delivered and stored everything in the barn. He ordered all new windows and doors, new kitchen cabinets and appliances. He had an electrician and plumber redoing everything since the old wires and piping had to be removed and replaced to meet new building codes.

Mildred ventured out one Saturday to inspect the progress. She found a man working on the tractor and another helping Henry put down new flooring in the house.

"It looks like you've found yourself a new hobby," she said when she found Henry.

"Yep, I'm keeping pretty busy." He was working from sun up to sunset every day and the progress was beginning to show. In another week, he'd be ready to move into the house.

Mildred had baked him an apple pie, and Henry stopped working long enough to enjoy a piece. He saved some of the crust for Wolf.

"You know, Mildred, you're the only person I've met who hasn't asked me for something. You are a kind lady and I'd like to do something nice for you."

"There's nothing I really need."

"Well, I was thinking about that old car of yours. A new one would eliminate worrying about repairs for a few years."

"That's true, but you don't have to spend any of your money on me; I'll manage just fine. I always have."

"Consider it my way of saying thank you for being a true friend. You rescued me when I needed it most, and you never asked for a dime, even after knowing I won the lottery."

"You gave me money for groceries, and you replaced the old stove. That was more than generous."

"One day next week let's you and me go car shopping. Let's see if we can't trade your old Buick in on something you'll like better."

"You still don't have a phone do you?"

"Nope, and I see no reason to have one."

"What if you get sick?"

"Then I'll drag my sorry ass over to the walk-in clinic and let them give me some pills."

"Well, I worry about you."

"Thanks, it's nice that someone worries, but please don't. Some evening, after this project is finally finished, I'll have you out for pizza to celebrate."

"Would you mind if I asked Cindy and the kids to come along, too?"

"Mildred, just stop, okay? Cindy is a very attractive woman who is much younger than me. She won't have trouble finding someone, even if it takes a while. First, she has to dump that jerk she's living with."

"But what about companionship, don't you ever get lonely?"

"Not since Wolf arrived. We keep each other company just fine."

"So you really like living like a hermit?"

"As a matter of fact I do. I've been a loner most of my life."

Mildred wished she were fifteen years younger. Then she would have shown Henry what he was missing. She had to admit that she'd enjoyed having Henry with her, even though it wasn't for very long. Now, once again, she was all alone. Somehow the place felt emptier than before.

Later that night Henry woke to a noise that sounded like a car coming down the driveway. Wolf was already alert, his ears were standing up and he was growling softly. Whoever it was stopped halfway down the drive. Henry crawled out of his sleeping bag and crept to the open barn door. He couldn't see any lights.

He listened carefully for a car door to close. Whoever it was, he was being quiet and didn't want his arrival to be noticed. Finally, Henry thought he heard someone walking toward the house. He estimated it was early morning, too early for sunrise and too early for any of the workmen to arrive. So it was an intruder, and intruders always meant trouble. Henry had an advantage however. He wasn't inside the house where he'd be expected to be sleeping. Another week and he would be.

Henry always left the sliding barn door partly open so Wolf could enter or leave as needed. Henry slipped out, grabbing a large crowbar and motioning for Wolf to be silent. Somehow the dog seemed to understand and followed Henry out of the barn without making a sound.

Ironically, a new door and lock had already been installed, but there was no reason yet to lock the new front door.

In the dark, Henry could barely make out a figure at the front door, standing on the freshly-painted porch.

The front door popped open, the new rubber seal made a slight noise like a hiss. Henry and Wolf stayed clear of the house, keeping the door in view. Now the intruder was inside and Henry saw a small cone of light from a high-intensity flashlight moving across his newly-tiled hallway.

It was decision time: Henry could either confront the intruder in the house or he could proceed quietly up the driveway to the parked vehicle where he'd let the air out of several tires, preventing an easy escape. Then he could come back and deal with the intruder, which he decided was the better plan.

The vehicle was a black four-door sedan. Henry found it unlocked. A quick inspection of the glove box revealed a loaded .38-calibre revolver. Henry took it, wondering why the intruder didn't have it with him, unless he had another gun and didn't feel the need to carry both. There was a police scanner and a portable flashing red light unit, the type cops used when driving unmarked cars. And there was a two-way radio mounted under the dash. The car was registered to LaMarr Puckett.

Henry should have known that after the auction LaMarr would continue to give him grief. Henry proceeded to let the air out of both rear tires. Then an impulsive thought hit him. He went back inside the car, examined the radio to make sure how it worked, keyed the mic and said, "Hello, anyone listening to this please call the police and report a break-in at Fowler's Ranch Road. It's the last house at the end of the road."

"Who is this?" someone replied when Henry released the mic button.

Henry didn't bother to respond. Someone had heard his message. That was enough for someone on duty to investigate.

He was still carrying the crowbar and had a few minutes before a police cruiser would arrive. Using the crowbar, Henry smashed the windshield, then the rear window. The noise was exceptionally loud. Henry and Wolf ran into the nearby stand of trees and waited in the darkness.

LaMarr was running toward his car yelling, "Who's out there? I've got a gun!"

With his flashlight, LaMarr was inspecting the broken windows and flat tires when a police cruiser came down the driveway with the light bar flashing. A spotlight focused on LaMarr's damaged car.

"Hey, is that you, LaMarr?" a voice called out from the patrol car.

Henry and Wolf remained hidden in the trees. And they were still there when the tow truck arrived to hook onto LaMarr's car an hour later. The sun was just rising.

"What the hell you doin' out here this time of night?" the tow truck driver asked. It was the same question the officer asked LaMarr earlier. LaMarr had fashioned a flimsy excuse, that he was investigating a suspicious incident involving his girlfriend. He thought she might be shacked-up with the rags-to-riches guy who now lived here, so he came out to check.

"Did you see her car out here?" the officer asked earlier.

"No, but that doesn't prove anything," LaMarr responded.

"So did you catch them doing anything nasty?"

"No, but they probably heard me coming."

"This is gonna be tough to explain, LaMarr. I think you better call your girlfriend and see if she's home. Want me to do it?"

"No, I'll handle it." He had sat in the patrol car and waited for the tow truck to arrive. Henry couldn't hear any more of their conversation and it didn't matter.

Later that morning, as Henry pulled out of his drive onto Fowler's Ranch Road, a police cruiser suddenly appeared with its light bar flashing. It was LaMarr getting out of the cruiser. This time he was in uniform. He'd been waiting.

"Okay, shit for brains, let's see your driver's license and registration." He was grinning. "That is, if you have one. My computer says you don't."

"Been waiting here long?" Henry asked through the open window. Wolf was barking from the back of the truck, ready to attack. "Wolf, stay!" Henry said.

"Long enough. I'm sending you the bill for the damage you did to my car."

"What damage? I didn't hit anyone." Henry was leaning over to get the registration from the glove box.

"I know what you did and you'll pay for that stunt, I guarran-damn-tee ya. Good thing I didn't catch you in the act or I would've shot you. Think about that asshole."

"Was that your car that was towed from my drive earlier this morning?"

"Yes, and you know it was! And you also know that there's a big hurt waiting for you, pulling a stupid stunt like that. I'm one of those guys who holds a grudge a long time. In fact, I'm gonna be your worst nightmare before this is over."

"Well, seeing as how you seem to have it in for me, and seeing that you seem to feel free to visit me in the wee hours of the morning without an invitation, causes me to wonder if I should be fearing for my life?"

"Maybe you should." LaMarr's wide grin suddenly turned to surprise when he saw that Henry was pointing a .38 pistol at him. It was the same pistol Henry had taken from LaMarr's glove box. The serial number had been scratched away, making it an illegal weapon and probably not registered to LaMarr.

It didn't take a lot of effort to subdue LaMarr with Wolf there snarling. Henry handcuffed him to the steering wheel of the cruiser. Using the radio, Henry called, "Hello, anyone listening, please send the sheriff out to Fowler's Ranch Road again to collect this stupid deputy who keeps threatening me because he lost the bid at the auction."

"That's bull shit!" LaMarr screamed.

His gun and his keys were on the back seat, out of reach. Henry disconnected the mic, preventing another call. Without LaMarr noticing, he slipped the .38 pistol under the driver's seat to be found sometime later, without Henry's fingerprints. Let LaMarr explain that one.

"Invade my privacy again and that hurt you mentioned will arrive in a most unexpected manner. This is your last and only warning." Henry spoke softly to make his point. There was no need to yell and no witnesses to the conversation.

"You're crazy," LaMarr yelled after Henry.

"Ah, you finally got it right, LaMarr. Add dangerous to crazy and that would make me a very dangerous man! Don't show up here again or you just might get buried on your grandfather's old farm."

Henry drove down his driveway, parking behind the barn so the truck was out of sight. With the truck back on his property and not the road, LaMarr had no real justification for stopping him. The question would be what was LaMarr doing out here.

Now Henry had to get a driver's license and register the truck. All the documentation he'd hoped to avoid. He wanted to remain anonymous. He didn't want people to know where he lived. With that philosophy in mind, he refused to install a mailbox. Whatever mail he did get, he'd collect at the post office. All he really wanted was privacy.

Sleeping in a Cardboard Box

"Marie, for the hundredth time, tell me why that kid can't put on some clothes. He lies around here all weekend in his pajamas, watching stupid cartoons and gorging himself on potato chips. He looks like an overweight blob." Wilson was tired of yelling at his eleven year-old son, Howard, who ignored him. The kid showed no fear of and no respect for his father.

"Stop picking on him. And stop talking about him like that while he's in the room," Marie shouted. It was becoming an unnerving ritual between them.

It hardly made any difference. Wilson had vowed years ago not to lay a hand on the kid again after a much-needed spanking that left blisters. Now he was tempted to break that vow. Whenever Wilson banished Howie from the living room couch, Howie quickly found a substitute spot on their bed in front of a smaller screen TV. It used to worry Wilson that the kid didn't seem to have any friends.

In the past year he'd washed his hands of most parenting and left things to his wife, who coddled the kid. It was a constant irritant to him. Now he chose to battle with his wife in a different manner, talking about the kid as if he weren't there. It was a weak attempt to embarrass Howie and his mother at the same time.

Daylight Savings Time arrived recently, causing the clocks to be turned back an hour, so it got dark much earlier. Wilson hated coming home from work when it was already dark. It put him in a foul mood. That mood didn't improve when he'd find Howie stretched out on the couch, munching chips like a squirrel getting ready for winter. Howie was their only child for which Wilson was grateful. Two like him would push Wilson over the edge.

Lately, Wilson had been giving a lot of thought to his present circumstances. He'd fallen short of the goals he'd set for himself ten years earlier. His classmates from college were in managerial positions while he was delivering furniture for a discount house. His marketing degree was totally wasted, a fact that Marie mentioned at inconvenient times. Their circle of friends seemed to diminish to a smaller group every year. Being a married man had become an obligation without any of the benefits. He often thought of leaving one morning and never returning. He doubted he'd be missed. The more he thought about it, the more intrigued he became.

Six months ago, Wilson brought home a king-sized bed and mattress. It was a returned piece, so he got it at a bargain. It didn't take long for him to realize the mistake he'd made. Marie slept on the far end, so far away she could have been in another bedroom. It didn't improve the romance as he'd hoped. Instead it separated them even more. About the same time he discovered that instead of paying off the monthly charge accounts, Marie had been making token payments, allowing the balances to climb higher each month. That's when Wilson took a firm stand demanding that she get a part-time job to help with the bills.

At 44, Marie still considered herself attractive. She'd maintained her figure, well enough to still fit into a size eight dress and get looks whenever they went out to dinner, which wasn't often. She got a part-time job as a sales clerk in the women's fashions section of J.C. Penney and proceeded to spend her paychecks on makeup and clothes. She didn't feel it was her fault that Wilson didn't bring home enough to pay all the mounting bills. The fact that they were three months behind on the mortgage payments didn't bother her. She never liked the house and liked it less each day. If the bank wanted it, they could have it. She'd been thinking about moving out.

A cute younger girl, recently divorced, and also working part-time at Penney's, hinted she was looking for a roommate to help with the rent. Marie had no doubts that the girl would snag a boyfriend soon and that might complicate the living arrangements. However, Marie considered it as one of her options. If she could snag a prosperous boyfriend, her worries about bills would be solved. She felt she was long overdue for some romantic adventure. Her head was filled with fantasies.

With a wife who no longer loved him and a fat, obnoxious son he no longer liked, Wilson started considering his options. He didn't see anything positive in the future, just more bills and aggravation. For brief periods during the day, while driving, he considered just walking away from it all. Leave the house, the job, the area, and start over fresh somewhere new. The dream continued to get more and more detailed as he kept going back to it.

The problem was, he wasn't an adventurous person and he really didn't know anyplace where he could make a new start. But the idea appealed to him. Someplace where it was warm all the time would be nice.

His first step toward a new life happened unexpectedly while carrying cardboard boxes to the back of the store where he'd collapse them and put them into a huge dumpster behind the building next to the loading dock.

"Hey, mister, you got any refrigerator boxes you want to get rid of?"

The man startled him. He was obviously homeless. He was wearing two coats and pushing a shopping basket from the market next door. It appeared that he had all his worldly possessions in that basket.

"I can save one for you," Wilson replied.

"Frigidaire has the best boxes. See if you can find one of those. Look for one of their twenty cubic inch models."

Wilson just shook his head. Not only did the man need a box for shelter, he was particular about what kind of box.

"When should I come by for it?" The homeless man asked.

"I don't know, maybe tomorrow afternoon. Stop back then."

"Could you make it later today? It's supposed to rain tonight and I got to waterproof it so I won't get soaked."

Wilson wondered where the man lived. He hadn't seen him around, so perhaps he was just passing through the area. Wilson made a mental note to keep the delivery truck locked. While he felt sorry for the man, he didn't want anything stolen.

That night it rained, in fact it poured, and Wilson hadn't found a suitable refrigerator box. He woke during the night wondering where a person would find shelter in such conditions. He decided to make a special effort in the morning to find the man a suitable box, maybe throw in an old tarp and a furniture blanket. No one would miss those items. Wilson lay there, half-awake, listening to the rain and wondering what it must be like to sleep in a cardboard box outside in the cold, wet weather. It had to be a terrible way to exist, yet it couldn't be much worse than the way Wilson was currently living. The overdue bills weighed heavily on him. Soon, they'd be forced to leave their home of fifteen years. He'd start to look around for a furnished room to rent. Marie and Howie could fend for themselves. It might even teach both of them a good lesson. And, maybe, just maybe, they'd appreciate what they once had.

The next morning Wilson left for work early, then stopped by McDonald's for coffee and a breakfast sandwich. He went directly to the warehouse area and began to search for the largest cardboard carton he could find. He wrestled it to the loading dock area and opened the back door hoping to see the homeless man waiting. Eventually, around 10:30, after it had stopped raining, the man appeared.

"Here's the box you ordered," Wilson said with a smile.

"Looks good. Now I gotta find a way to drag it to where my stuff is hidden. You do deliveries?"

"Depends on where I'd have to drop it off. Where are you staying?"

"Well, it was the Ritz until they found out I didn't have any credit. Heh, heh." The man laughed. "Actually they profiled me, decided I was adding a foul smell to the reception area and kicked me out. I've been removed from a lot of classy places."

None of them around here, Wilson thought. This was a small town with a few motels. The nearest thing to an upscale restaurant was Applebee's. Never-the-less, Wilson had to smile about the way the man seemed to handle his plight.

"So how's it goin' with you, Bud?" The homeless man asked.

"My name is Wilson."

"Yeah, well I call everyone Bud. That way I don't have to remember names. I like to keep everything as basic as possible."

"You call women Bud too?"

"No, I call 'em all Rosebud. That way they don't get offended, like when you make the mistake and call one of 'em hon."

"So what do I call you?"

"You can call me Sam."

"That your real name?"

"No, but you can still call me Sam. My real name got lost somewhere and I no longer need it. I'm a drop-out from society. I don't vote and there's no record of me ever existing, except at the shelter."

"So the homeless shelter knows who you are?"

"Sort of. They recognize me when I show up for a meal and a shower. I just put down Sam on the sign-in sheet. If they need a last name, they can put down whatever they want, I don't care. That's the story of my life in a nutshell: I just don't care about anything or anybody."

"Somehow I don't believe that. Surely you cared about someone once upon a time."

"I had a wife once. Nice lady. I tried to give her everything and still it wasn't enough, know what I mean? Eventually she met a guy who promised her the moon, with a fence around it, and she fell for it, leaving me with a stack of bills. I had to file for bankruptcy. I started drinking and never stopped until I ran out of money and wore out my welcome."

"So how long have you been homeless?"

"I don't keep track of time. Don't own a watch either. If I

had to make a guess, I'd say five years, give or take."

Wow, that was a long time to live like Sam. Wilson wasn't sure he could live like that for more than a month or so, and certainly not in cold weather conditions.

"If I were in your shoes, Sam, I think I'd make my way down to Florida, where the weather is warmer at least."

"Yeah, I do that. I go back and forth when it suits me. Right now there are too many just like me living in Florida. It's becoming dangerous in some places like Tampa. They're putting up tents in the parks."

"That doesn't sound so bad. Better than a cardboard box isn't it?"

"It's obvious you don't know the first thing about it. You got any coffee in there? I could use a cup."

Wilson left the loading dock, went into the office. and started a pot of coffee. He was ready for another cup. While he waited for the coffee to brew, he thought about what Sam had said. It was true: he didn't know much about being homeless. Until now, he hadn't given it much thought. Existing like Sam had to be the very worst of all situations. Wilson wondered if he could handle it as well.

When the coffee was ready, he took both cups back to the loading dock. Sam was sitting there waiting.

"What did you have for breakfast?" Sam asked.

"I was in a hurry this morning so I stopped by McDonald's and had a breakfast sandwich and a cup of coffee."

"See how lucky you are that you can do that? I just had a piece of stale bread I was saving. I didn't think you'd bring me anything."

"Look, are you interested in making a few bucks? I could use someone to help me deliver some furniture today."

"Bud, I appreciate the offer, but I gotta say no. Work isn't my thing anymore. Look at me. Take a good hard look. You think some young housewife is gonna want to see me tracking into her house looking like I do? Get real. I'm a drop-out from society and that's by choice. People and me, we just don't see eye to eye anymore. I did my time, came home and wished I hadn't. End of story."

It was a lot for Wilson to digest. Behind all the facial hair, and the rags, there was another human being who'd experienced a world of hurt and abuse. Wilson wished he had more time to ask more questions, but he had things to do. The day had begun, and he was needed elsewhere. Sam told him where he'd like the cardboard box dropped off. It was a parking lot on the south edge of town surrounded on two sides by a wooded area.

That night when Wilson arrived home he found the place basically empty. The television set from the living room was gone, as were several pieces of furniture and all of Marie and Howard's clothes. It was obvious they'd moved out. A note on the kitchen counter said, *It's all yours.*

On top of the bills was an eviction notice from the bank. He had until the end of the month to remove his possessions and vacate the property. It was being turned over for auction. If he wasn't gone by the end of the month, the sheriff would get involved, to assist in his departure.

The refrigerator was empty except for some old cheese and a half-quart of milk past expiration. He found some crackers in the pantry along with some cereal. That would become his dinner. While he ate, he considered Sam's plight and thought about how close he was to being in the same boat, or box. Sam had nothing, yet he wasn't worried about anything. In contrast,

Wilson still had his old pickup truck, a few tools, and some clothes. And he still had a job along with a lot of worries and bills. *So who was better off?* he asked himself. With Marie and Howard gone, he was essentially starting over. While he had often considered being single again, the reality of it scared him a little.

Having met Sam, at least, he knew what the bottom looked like. Wilson still had a chance to get it right this next time around. He wasn't ready to sleep in a cardboard box and eat stale bread. Not if he could help it. With this new perspective he saw everything, including the recent past, in a new light. Suddenly the future looked promising. Every time he discarded a large appliance box, he'd think of Sam's plight and appreciate the remaining few things he still owned.

Starting Over

Travis woke with his usual dull hangover and dry mouth, not sure what day it was. He squinted at his watch then looked over at Donna, his sometime girlfriend. She was still sleeping, lightly snoring, with her back to him. A decision hung there waiting: curl up close, mess around, and be late for work again, or get up. He thought about work then remembered he no longer had that job. He'd been fired two days ago for being late too many times. That memory soured his mood for waking Donna. Instead Travis stretched, scratched his naked butt, and headed for the bathroom. He needed to pee then have a cigarette and strong coffee, in that order. Maybe then his mood would improve.

Maneuvering through the mess in the living room of Donna's aging singlewide mobile home, Travis reminded himself, for perhaps the hundredth time, that keeping a clean house wasn't a high priority for Donna. His presence didn't help; it was a convenient place to sleep and hang out with his buddies while Donna was working.

Sometimes his friends would crash, sleeping on the sagging couch or on the floor. It was Travis's job to throw out all the empty beer cans. They went directly out the back door onto a growing pile he called Mount Trashmore. The neighbors never complained because it wasn't any of their business, which was the best way to keep things peaceful.

And they never complained about his rusting old Ford

pickup that hadn't moved from the yard in six months. It needed brakes, new wheel bearings, and a transmission. The cost to repair it exceeded its total value. It represented a good summary of Travis's life for the past couple years; like the truck, he needed a complete overhaul.

Plopping down on the broken couch, Travis pulled on faded jeans and old boots that even The Salvation Army would refuse. He found Donna's purse and searched through her wallet. She was a waitress at Liberty's only cafe and made decent tips. He knew she usually kept a twenty hidden away somewhere. He found it. It would be enough to buy a sausage biscuit, a pack of smokes, and some gas for his aging motorcycle. Like Donna, it was no longer the sweet ride it once was. Travis wasn't big on philosophy, but every once in a while he'd reflect on his situation and his surrounding circumstances. Standing in the doorway, he realized the truck had become a metal yard ornament. It was one of just a few possessions that kept him anchored here. Donna hadn't complained about the truck. As long as it remained, she figured so would Travis.

He left the front door ajar so his departure would be as quiet as possible. He pushed his motorcycle down the hard-packed dirt road to the highway before starting it, afraid he'd wake Donna. Her two kids, by a previous marriage, were currently staying with her mother, and that was fine with Travis. It meant fewer mouths to feed and a lot less noise. And more room in the fridge for beer. He hadn't bothered to look, but he was pretty sure he'd finished the last of the beer.

Roaring down the highway, feeling the wind blasting him, always gave Travis a feeling of momentary freedom.

"Some days are better than others," he shouted above the engine noise. It was his daily mantra as he tried to decide what he was going to do with the rest of his life. First, he had to get past the morning. Then the rest of the day would fall into place. At twenty-eight, Travis was a fair carpenter. He could also lay brick and block, and he could lay Donna just about anytime he took a notion. His drinking buddies frequently joked that he got laid and laid off more than anyone they knew.

Tomorrow is Just Another Road

Merle Whitaker was also enjoying a similar sparkling crisp morning while driving west along Highway 70, just outside Liberty. He had the driver's side window down so he could smell the honeysuckle that lined parts of the road. Merle's new Buick was cruising along at a steady forty-five miles per hour, below the speed limit. He wasn't in any hurry. He was leaving Liberty for the last time without any thoughts of returning soon.

After his wife, Norma, died, he realized that most of their friends were really her friends, so he had little reason to remain living there alone. He sold the house, gave away a ton of old memories rather than having a yard sale, and said goodbye to his few remaining friends, promising to keep in touch. His worldly possessions were reduced to what was packed into two new suitcases and two cardboard boxes. Deciding what to keep was the challenging part. Also difficult was the realization that he no longer needed all those things he'd kept for so many years. He had all the memories locked away in his head. That was enough.

Merle had closed out the bank account, not sure where he'd deposit the money. He had a cashier's check in his jacket pocket for $196,000. He also had $5,000 in Traveler's Checks plus $600 in his wallet, along with his Discover card. He was headed in the general direction of the Gulf Coast where he hoped to find a place near the water to his liking and start over. He and Norma used to visit that area between Biloxi and Gulfport in the past, hitting a few casinos, playing the nickel slots and enjoying the sumptuous buffets. He'd heard they were rebuilding down there in the aftermath of Hurricane Katrina. With any luck he might find a bargain.

Now at seventy-four, without any family, the thought of embarking on a new adventure this late in his life was a little scary. This was the first trip he'd taken without Norma sitting in the passenger seat, helping with the navigation and reminding him where to turn. He missed Norma terribly. He even missed the petty arguments they occasionally had. And, he missed the turn-off that served as a short cut to get over to Interstate 65, allowing him to bypass all the busy Nashville traffic.

When they did argue, Norma was the one who was right most

often, he reflected. Merle found it easier to admit that now that she was gone. He wondered what she would have said about buying the new Buick. Probably that he didn't need a new car, which was true. It was an impulsive decision, something to make him feel better, lift his spirits. Heck, he didn't have to justify anything he did to anyone anymore. He was free to do as he pleased, yet he knew deep down that he was also lonely and afraid.

Every few minutes Merle would glance around and admire the blue leather seats, brushing his free hand over them. This was his first new car in many years and he was still learning how some of the features worked. He really liked the automatic door locks and the remote trunk release. As Merle reached over for the map on the seat beside him, he felt a slight pain in his chest. Heartburn he thought, and reached into his pocket for an antacid tablet. Soon he was sweating, even with the window down. Merle loosened his tie and unbuttoned his jacket. He was feeling uncomfortable and thought about pulling over to rest.

Merle was approaching a long curve so he'd have to wait for a convenient place to pull off the road. Here he was with a full tank of gas, no definite destination, no deadline to meet, and suddenly he was feeling nervous. His hands began to shake and he told himself to calm down and slow down. His chest began to tighten and he found it harder to breath. He saw a place to pull over and turned in that direction, then he passed out. Sometime later, he regained consciousness long enough to stare through the steering wheel and read the odometer. It read 1,068 miles. *I won't need an oil change for at least another 2,000 miles,* he thought as he slumped over onto the beautiful blue leather seat. The Buick had rolled to a stop in a clump of trees. The engine finally quit when the gas tank emptied.

Travis crammed a sausage biscuit into his mouth and gulped down two cups of black coffee, the second cup being a free refill at Fred's Mini-Mart. He felt impatient even though he didn't have anyplace in particular to go. Fred reminded

Travis that he still owed him $40 and wondered when he might get his money; Fred knew about Travis getting fired. Everyone in Liberty already knew he'd been fired. It was a small two gas station community, another reason Travis thought about moving on. Everyone knew too much about him and everyone else living there.

"Why don't you check out some of the builders over in Lebanon?" Fred asked. "I hear they're building a lot of houses over there."

"Hey, don't worry about your money, Freddy. I'll have me another job soon enough and pay you back." Travis had known Fred for the past five years, which was as long as he'd been in Liberty, and longer than he'd been anywhere else. He thought of himself as a modern-day gypsy.

"I know. But you need to give some thought to the future. You planning on sticking with that gal you're shacked up with?"

"Funny you would mention that, Freddy. I've been thinking it's time I got my act together and did something else. I just need a break." He guessed Lebanon was as good a place as any to start looking around.

Travis kicked his old Honda into life and roared on down the road in the direction of Lebanon, twenty miles away. People often commented that Liberty was in the middle of nowhere, and Travis always agreed with them. After ten minutes going 70 mph, Travis felt the two cups of coffee working on him. He needed to make a quick pit stop. He pulled over at a wide spot at the end of a long curve, parked his bike, and walked toward the bushes, following recent tire tracks.

He was surprised to find a shiny silver Buick parked between two trees, hidden from the road. Cautiously Travis walked to the car. He looked into the open driver's side window and saw a man's body slumped over on the seat. Travis had no idea how long the car had been there. His only clue was all the flies and the terrible smell coming from inside the car. The apparent dead body was an older, bald man who appeared well-dressed.

Reluctantly, Travis opened the door and searched the car and body. He found the man's wallet containing $640. He also found the cashier's check and traveler's checks. Travis knew there was something different about this day when he'd left Donna's place this morning. He'd suddenly found his ticket to a new start. Meanwhile, he'd let someone else discover the body and the car. He wasn't interested in any of the items in the trunk. None of the clothes were his size.

His first stop in Lebanon was a barbershop, where he got a shampoo and had his hair styled. Next, he spent an hour in J.C. Penney's picking out some new clothes. It felt good to be able to pay cash.

Fred was surprised when Travis walked into the Mini-Mart later that same day.

"Hey, Freddy, guess what? It's me, Travis. Bet you're wondering what happened, huh?" Travis put two twenties on the counter, payment of his overdue debt.

"Well, I don't hear any sirens, so I guess you didn't rob a bank. What's going on?"

"I took your advice and went over to Lebanon. I decided I needed to clean up a little if I was going to get a decent job. It's amazing what new clothes and a haircut can do for a man's image and self-esteem. I also talked to the manager at Lowe's. I asked him if any of the builders that came in were looking for help. Guess what?"

"I'm going to guess the manager offered you a job instead," Fred said.

"Bingo. When he learned I had building experience, he said he needed someone in the contractor sales department. That's where I'm starting, first thing tomorrow morning."

"Good for you. I hope it works out, Travis."

"Yeah, me too. I didn't want to leave here owing you money."

"What about your girlfriend, Donna?"

"I think I'll just let her keep my old truck. That way she'll have something to remember me by." Travis laughed, thinking the truck would probably sit there forever, dying with all the other decaying yard ornaments in the park.

Tomorrow is Just Another Road

Travis could remember thinking Donna was the kind of woman who looked good after 11:00 PM in a redneck bar. She once bragged that she hadn't paid for a drink in the last four years. Travis had never bothered to correct her on that one. There were different ways to pay. He'd go back to her place, knowing that she'd already be at work, and leave a note along with the keys to the truck, and return the twenty he'd taken. He estimated that it would take her about three days to get over him before she found another guy promising her better things. Yeah, right. If he remembered correctly, he had been leaning on the bar, his face close to hers when he whispered, "Honey, some days are better than others, and you are making this a fine day for me." His crooked smile had done the trick and she kissed him. He drove her home that night in his old pick-up truck where it still remained.

By the time Travis arrived back at Donna's trailer, she was gone. There was a note telling him to stop by the restaurant if he wanted something to eat.

For the first time in ages, Travis wasn't interested in having a beer or a free meal. He gulped down a glass of water instead and looked into the bathroom mirror. He liked what he saw smiling back. It was the best he'd felt about himself in years. He had a plan and decided to stick with it. He was tired of being a loser: been there, done that. The dead guy in the Buick had given him a second chance; it was his ticket to the future.

"Some days sure are better than others," he yelled as he left Liberty for the last time. Heading west toward Lebanon, Travis was doing the exact same thing Merle Whitaker tried to do: start over.

Bayou Boogie Blues

Ely's real name was Ellis, but he never used it. Thought it sounded like a girl's name. His last name was Jenks, and he hadn't used that in a long time, not since he was known as Staff Sergeant Jenks during Desert Storm. A few clowns tried spelling his name as jinx and learned a new meaning for hurt. Fast forward to the present and Katrina became *the storm* to change his life for good. He'd known women who could break your heart, but this old gal tore out his soul, leaving him with just the clothes on his back. And a few overdue debts.

Just about everyone got wiped out along the Gulf Coast, a place Ely had called home for forty-three years. Bay St. Louis and Pass Christian were his stomping grounds: where he fished, drank, worked, made bets and whored around. Everyone knew Ely and knew he liked to party hard. If he'd ever learned to play a decent guitar, he could have passed himself off as a younger version of his idol, Jimmy Buffet, but with more hair. His friends joked that he had a new girlfriend every other payday, which wasn't too far off the mark. Sally was his latest, but she blew the area at the first hurricane warnings, leaving him alone to decide whether to stick it out or leave. Her leaving told him something about their relationship; it was too casual, not solid enough to hold together.

Like many other situations caught by the storm, he had waited too long. His truck was sitting in water that was over the tires and rising. Even if it had started, he couldn't drive it anywhere. Ely knew he would have to leave and travel light. He found an old canvas backpack, and he threw in a few clothes and the money he had stashed away to hold him over between jobs. A neighbor came by in a small fishing boat and picked him up. Navigating was difficult because of downed trees, poles, and wires. He hated to leave the house that once belonged to his parents. All his earlier memories were stored there, including family pictures.

Now it was time to move on, but the *where to* was uncertain. Things didn't look any better to the west, where Katrina did even more damage. So he headed east, toward Florida, hitching rides and walking, mostly walking. Everywhere he looked, all he could see was devastation. The beautiful beaches were gone. So were the grand old homes that faced the water. Fishing boats were in permanent dry dock inland, on their sides or upside down, broken like match sticks. All the piers were gone. Hollywood couldn't make a horror film to compare with it. Ely wondered how long it would be before things ever got back to normal. Years probably. He knew he'd come back eventually.

The upside of leaving was the money he still owed Juicy LaFollet. He hadn't planned to skip out, but with the storm coming, he couldn't work and couldn't pay any bills. Juicy was no doubt having similar problems trying to collect, looking for people who'd already left. Ely was pretty sure that the last balance on Juicy's books was no more than $1,300. Of course Juicy would add on some outrageous interest.

When Ely arrived in Biloxi he discovered it had also been hit and badly damaged. The flood water was so high that parts of the highway were closed. Ely detoured over to I-10, hoping for a ride as far as Pensacola, then on to Jacksonville. That was the plan. From there he'd work his way south and hope to find work.

Peaches Meriwether refused to believe she was past her prime at fifty-two. When she looked at herself, in that full-length cheval mirror, she still saw a younger woman with a full figure. Deep down, she knew that giving in to her vices contributed to her expanded plus dress size. Her vices were chocolates, cheesecake, Grey Goose Vodka martinis, and younger men. She knew all about men and their secret desires. She first learned from her abusive step-father and, later, when she left home soon after graduating high school in Baton Rouge, she learned a lot more when she arrived in New Orleans, out of money. Fortunately, the city of many sins provided her a steady income for more than thirty years. Peaches started out working the streets, then moved into an established bordello where she later became a madam. In a manner of speaking, she'd seen and done it all. Over the years, she'd made some influential friends. She had an elite clientele and an excellent reputation.

Peaches was visiting her older sister in Biloxi when Katrina came barging into the area with category five winds. She'd been nursing a terrible hangover and delayed her return trip to New Orleans until she felt better. Then the hurricane changed her plans.

When the storm hit, Peaches took a quick mental inventory. She had two large suitcases packed with clothes and all her expensive jewelry in the bottom of her makeup case. Her aging pink Cadillac had a full tank of gas, enough to get her to Mobile, where the storm damage was reported to be much less. She didn't want to venture too far from New Orleans. She owned a dozen small rental houses and there would be insurance claims to file as soon as the storm passed and people were allowed to go home again. The clean-up would take weeks and maybe longer, depending on the damage.

Traffic was bumper-to-bumper waiting to get onto I-10. While waiting in stalled traffic, she spotted a man walking with a backpack, going in the same direction, periodically sticking his thumb out. Peaches wasn't afraid of strangers. She had a nickel-plated .38 in the glove box, fully loaded. If she ever needed to use it, she wouldn't have to waste time fumbling around trying to load the damned thing. Not since her step-father had a man ever taken advantage of her: physically, emotionally, or financially. That experience had given her all the motivation to survive.

"I'll give you a lift, but I can't guarantee how far we'll get," Peaches said through the open window. Rain had slacked-off a little.

"I appreciate it, but I hate to sit on your white leather seat since I'm soaked through," Ely said.

"Honey, that's the least of my worries right now. Where are you headed?"

"Right now, whereever you're going is fine with me. This storm has wiped me out. I lost a home and truck, not to mention a good job."

"Yeah, well, you're still breathing air and able to walk and take nourishment. Consider yourself lucky."

"The nourishment part needs work. I haven't eaten anything all day. You wouldn't happen to have a candy bar handy would you?"

"Check the back seat. There's a small cooler. Take out two, one for you and one for me. See how lucky you are?" Peaches was trying to estimate the man's age. He looked fit, but he definitely needed a shave.

"I think you may have saved my life. Thank you." Ely tried to eat slowly savoring the candy bar. "My name's Ely and I'm from Pass Christian."

"Oh yeah? My name is Peaches and I know a lot of men from that area. They're clients so to speak."

"Really? What are you, a beautician?"

"That's not a bad guess, Honey. No, I'm in the flesh trade. I own a stable of young ladies who can *curl* your hair and put a big smile on your face."

"No kidding. Where is your place?

"Right now it's probably under water and my stable of young ladies will need to be replenished when I get back to New Orleans."

"Well, I'm not in a big hurry to get back there. You ever heard of a big fat guy they call Juicy? He's from New Orleans, too."

"Honey, I've known Juicy for a long time and I can tell you he's one bad dude. He tried to shake me down once and I almost put a bullet in him. He's always rough with my girls. I hope you don't owe him any money."

"Yeah, I do. I owe him for some gambling debts plus the interest, which is outrageous."

"Good luck and watch your back. He's mean as a snake. I'm actually surprised someone hasn't put him out of his misery by now."

After three hours in slow-moving traffic, Ely and Peaches had compared philosophies on just about everything. Peaches finally asked Ely how old he was and learned he was ten years younger than she, which put him in the right category, right up there with the chocolate. She had several bottles of Grey Goose tucked away in the trunk. She'd take one out later, whenever they found a place to stay for the night. After all, Ely owed her, and she planned to collect.

Mobile was getting drenched with rain and high winds, but they were not as destructive. Driving, however, took concentration. When Peaches saw neon lights on at a bar on the outskirts of town, she pulled into the parking lot. Despite the bad weather, there were quite a few patrons.

Ely ordered a steak and fries along with a long neck beer that he consumed in three swallows and then was ready for another. Peaches ordered the same, but she had a glass of wine instead of beer. They sat at a table and she sat across from Ely so she could scrutinize him closely.

"So what kind of work have you done in the past years since the army?" Her hands were folded under her chin in a cute pose.

"Actually, I've done a variety of things. I worked on shrimp boats for a while. That's hard work. The Cajuns do that job better than anyone. I drove a forklift truck in a warehouse until they told me I had to join the union. And I did some part-time bartending for a friend of mine who owns a small place near the water. I enjoyed that."

"Ever do any bouncer-type work?"

"Not as a job, but I've had to put a few guys out the door when they went over the limit and got nasty."

"Are you any good in a fight?"

"I can hold my own. Why the twenty questions?"

"I've got one more, but I'll save it for later." She wanted to know if he was any good in bed. Rather than ask, she'd find out first hand. So far she was intrigued by what she saw in this man who called himself Ely.

Two rounds of drinks later, Peaches decided to reveal the plan she had forming in her head. She examined Ely's knuckles on both hands much like a fortune-teller.

"It looks like you've done some rough work. I've got a proposition to make. I've got an escort business..."

"You mean you run a whorehouse."

"If you want to put it that way, yes. But I pride myself in providing good stock for my clients. The problem is, every once in a while I get some tough guy who isn't satisfied or who tries to beat up on one of my girls. I can't allow that to happen. Do you see where this is going?"

"You offering me a job to be a bouncer?"

"More like a bodyguard. You'd be my personal assistant. And, of course, you'd be protecting me as well as my girls. It would be easy work, good pay, and excellent side benefits! You'd be able to sample the goods from time to time."

"Does that include you?"

"You're very perceptive. I like that in a man. Yes, I have a few desires as well, I don't deny it. Just as long as you remember that I'm the one who pays you."

"Sounds great, but need I remind you that right now most of New Orleans is under water and it might be a few years before things get back to normal."

"I'm aware of that. Meanwhile we can start recruiting new stock. It won't take as long as you think before they'll start the re-building process. That means an influx of construction workers who will need some comfort and relaxation. I'll be providing that. In the meantime, you can start practicing being my personal bodyguard and chauffeur. You do have a valid driver's license don't you?"

"I haven't accepted the job yet."

"Oh, I think you will, Ely. And you'll do it very well. I intend to give you some personal instructions on how to treat a lady." Now all she needed was to find a decent motel for a few days so she could wear him out. She'd teach him how to boogie, even if he thought he knew how.

Ely thought about his good fortune. He'd just been offered a job when there were few to be had. And there was also the promise of more women than any man could ever want, if Peaches was being truthful. He knew she was playing him, and the picture she painted for him was probably too good to be true. She was a smart business woman—he had no doubts about that. And she wasn't bad looking, even if she was older than he was. That had never been a problem. He'd dated a few older women in the past.

He was willing to spend the night with her. After all, she was picking up the expenses and his schedule was definitely flexible. What he needed most was a shower, a good night's rest, a big breakfast in the morning, and a long ride to Jacksonville. He remembered his grandfather saying, "Too much of a good thing sometimes makes it a bad thing eventually." Ely had to agree with that wisdom. Peaches had an agenda that didn't exactly match his. And, he wasn't ready to go back to New Orleans and face the devastation waiting there. No, no. He preferred to face the unknown.

"I need a room for a few days," the fat man said, standing at the check-in desk. He was big and he was bald. His smile had a cruelness that made people feel uneasy.

"I'm terribly sorry, sir, but we're completely booked-up. It's the storm. You might find something outside Mobile."

"I guess I didn't phrase it right. I don't give a shit if you're booked-up, just give me a key to one of your rooms so I can get out of these wet clothes, take a shower, and get some sleep. If you have to kick someone out, do it!"

"Sir, I can't do that. I'm going to have to ask you to leave now."

"Yeah, well that don't cut it in my book. See, if you don't produce a key in the next two minutes, I'm going to break all the fingers on your right hand, the one you write and eat with."

The desk clerk hated confrontations. A threat of bodily harm made him break out in a sweat. He was sure the big man meant what he said. Uncertain what to do, he searched for a room that wasn't yet occupied. He found one that he was holding for someone who had made a reservation and hadn't arrived yet.

"See, that wasn't so hard, was it?"

"Uh, sir, if you don't mind, I'll need a credit card, or cash, whichever you prefer."

"I'll be down later to settle up with you; right now I need some sleep. And if you're thinkin' bout callin' the cops, think again, cause I'll know who sent them. Right now, they're busy with more important things. You get my drift?"

"Yes, yes sir. I hear you." The big man had read his mind. He was trouble, it was written all over his face and 300-pound body.

Four hours later, he was rested. Now he was hungry and decided to brave the rain to find a decent place to eat. He walked to his black Hummer, his pride and joy. He never ran anywhere, even in the rain. As he was backing out, he noticed a familiar car in the parking lot. It was an older model pink Cadillac and it belonged to an old acquaintance, Peaches. The only other pink Caddy he'd ever seen belonged to a woman who sold Mary Kay cosmetics. Juicy patronized Peaches's place from time to time and wondered what brought her over this way? *Probably the same thing that brought me here: the damned hurricane.* The storm was costing him a lot of money. People who owed him were disappearing, and some might never come back. Juicy pulled under the covered entrance and walked over to the counter. The same desk clerk was there looking extremely nervous. Juicy had that effect on people, even those he knew.

"Is your room alright?"

"Yeah. I got a question for you. What room is the lady who's driving that pink Cadillac sitting in the parking lot in? And don't even think about telling me you don't know."

"I believe she came in with her husband. They're staying in room two oh four, on the second floor. Would you like me to call their room?"

"No, they're old friends. I'll just knock on their door and take them out to dinner. So don't call their room, understand me?"

"Yes, sir." The desk clerk was wishing the man who worked

security had shown-up for work. The storm was wrecking everybody's schedule.

A few minutes later Juicy was pounding on the door of room 204. "Hey, Peaches, open up. It's your old pal, Juicy." He yelled it loud enough for anyone nearby to hear.

Ely and Peaches were in the shower. They heard the pounding on the door but couldn't make out what Juicy was yelling above the sound of the water and their respective moans.

"Well, lookie who's here!" Juicy exclaimed when the door opened to reveal Peaches with Ely standing next to her, both wrapped in towels. "Get dressed and we'll find someplace to eat. I'm starving. Hope I didn't interrupt something important," he chuckled, knowing he had and not caring. He'd managed to push his way inside the doorway.

"We're not hungry right now, Juicy. Thanks for the kind offer," Peaches said, hoping he'd leave, knowing he wouldn't.

"Yeah, well get dressed and come along and watch me eat then. You too, Ely. We got a lot to talk about, and since you owe me some money, I'm going to let you buy."

"Where's your sidekick, Nigel?" Ely asked, noting that Juicy was standing in the doorway alone.

Juicy was rarely seen without Nigel somewhere close by. Most people thought Nigel was a Brit, but he was actually an Australian. Nigel was tall, on the lanky side of lean with long shaggy hair that was always weeks beyond needing a haircut. He had nicotine-stained bad teeth, which he displayed whenever he smiled. It was a wicked smile that sent chills through most people who had the unfortunate experience of being in his presence. Nigel was Juicy's best collector.

Nigel collected overdue accounts for Juicy. His specialty was using a sharp knife. If you owed Juicy money, and you were late paying what you owed, you could expect a visit from Nigel. You could also expect a lot of pain and the loss of a fingertip. Nigel would cut off your index finger at the first joint, leaving a telltale reminder. Nigel then collected, and kept, the missing fingertips for his private collection. As a consequence very few people ever skipped making a payment. Nigel's reputation in and around New Orleans was legendary. His only loyalty was to Juicy.

"Nigel's on a special assignment. I don't need him right now."

Ely had to assume that Juicy hadn't shown up unexpectedly to collect the money he owed, otherwise Nigel would be standing in the vicinity with his notorious wicked grin.

Juicy told Ely to drive while he sat in the passenger seat and Peaches had the entire back seat. The interior of the Hummer was black leather.

"Know what I really like about this truck?" Juicy asked. "It will drive through water two feet high without any problem. Yes, I do love this truck!"

There were very few vehicles moving in the downpour. Ely spotted a Shoney's restaurant and, without asking, pulled into the parking lot.

"They better have some fried chicken." Juicy commented. He liked to eat with his fingers. He liked ribs and fried chicken. Both were on display in the buffet and he had heaped his plate with lots of each, disregarding Ely and Peaches while he ate, constantly licking his fingers and smacking his lips. Peaches couldn't look at him and Ely couldn't take his eyes away.

So far Juicy had made only a passing mention of the money owed. It was the shoe yet to be dropped and Ely realized he was holding his breath waiting. Peaches kept shooting him furtive looks. It was obvious she was worried as well. Neither of them ate anything.

"Okay, here's the deal. I've been thinking about this for some time, so running into you like this is fortunate." When no one spoke Juicy continued, "You run a classy operation, Peaches. You know a lot of prominent people and you keep your mouth shut. I like that. The skin game has always appealed to me. I guess you already know that since I've been one of your clients. Now I plan to be your silent partner."

"Thanks for the offer, but I'm not interested. I've got plans of my own."

"Yeah, well maybe I was a little hasty in the way I put it to you. See, I'm a lot like you. I know a lot of people, too. Some aren't as desirable as clients, but just like you, I'm in a cash business. I've been thinking about expanding for some time now and a good whorehouse fits in nicely."

"Juicy, I don't know how to put this politely, but I'm not interested in being partners with you. I don't even want you as a client."

"That's pretty blunt. You think you can get away talking to me like that because asshole here is gonna protect you? That ain't gonna happen. If you even think you're gonna do business back home, when things dry out, the only way will be with me as your partner. I can do it with or without you. With you fronting the operation, we'll get a better class of clientele, that's all."

"Like I said, not interested." Peaches finished her iced tea and started to get up from the booth, nodding at Ely that she was ready to leave.

"Sit down! I'm not finished. What you don't realize is I'm a very successful businessman. You only know me for the loan sharking. I also happen to own a string of storage units and a trucking company. Didn't know that, did you?"

"You keep talking in the present tense, like everything is still there waiting for you," Ely said. "News flash: it's all under water, if it's still there at all."

"I'm not worried about it, okay? This is a temporary interruption, that's all. In a few weeks, they'll have the water pumped out, people will be back at work, and I'll be right there supervising all my enterprises. We'll probably have to find you a new place," he said pointing a finger at Peaches.

"Juicy, you're not listening. And, you're not being realistic, either. It's going to take a long time to clean up the mess back there. Stop kidding yourself and get real."

"You want real? Here's real: I'm your new partner as of now. Tell your boy-toy here to pay me the money he owes me and then get lost. You got two double beds in that room, and I'm taking over one of them, and I don't plan to share. Got that?"

Ely got up and started walking toward the door. He had a key to the room and needed to gather up his stuff. He didn't plan to get in the middle of what Juicy had in mind. Peaches could deal with him.

Ely paid the bill and caught up with Juicy and Peaches at the door. Peaches was coming along reluctantly, if only because it was still pouring outside and she needed a ride back to the motel. All three of them got into the Hummer. This time Juicy was driving. The only sound was the wind and rain hitting the vehicle as they splashed through puddles on the road. Silence prevailed.

Juicy pulled under the overhang at the entrance to the motel. "Go up to the room, get your shit, and meet me back here in ten minutes. Don't make me come up and get you." Juicy reached across the seat to the glove box and took out a silver plated .45 caliber pistol. "If you run, I'll catch you. If I catch you, I'll kill you. Simple as that. You already owe me money, so it's just another business transaction to me. Now get out!"

Peaches was still in the back seat. She hadn't spoken a word. She knew this wasn't a good time to argue with Juicy. Ely only had a few minutes of freedom left and he had to use the time wisely. He had a key to the room. As soon as he opened the room door, he scanned the beds and table. Peaches had left her car keys on the dresser. He took them, along with his backpack, hurried down the back stairs and crossed the parking lot to her car.

Once inside, he opened the glove box and found her .38 caliber pistol. He was sure she would have one somewhere and he'd been right. He hurried back through the rear entrance, down the hall to the registration area, and walked out the front door to Juicy's waiting Hummer. Peaches was still in the back seat, looking pale.

"Took you long enough," Juicy said. "Get in." Then he pulled back into the rain and headed toward the highway. "After you cough up the fifteen hundred you owe me, I'll drop you off at the ramp to the Interstate. Maybe someone will take pity on you and give you a lift. Next time I see you, if I ever see you, you'd better stay out of my way. I'm giving you a pass this time, you understand? Now hand over the dough you owe me."

"I guess you don't think I could be useful to you," Ely said.

"What I think is you're a loser and I don't hang with losers. Consider yourself lucky that Nigel isn't here; he'd love to hurt you. He's the most sadistic sumbitch I've ever known and the best collector I've ever employed. Right now, he's chasing a couple of Mexicans who rented a storage unit from me."

"You sent him to collect storage rent?"

"No, I sent him after the truckload of weed that was stored in my unit. He missed them by just a few minutes. He may have caught up with them by now since they don't know he's following them."

"Why don't I get out here?" Ely could see the signs for Interstate 10. He had his hand on the door handle. Peaches' pistol was in his right hand pocket hidden from Juicy's view. Once he had the door open, he'd turn, pull the pistol, and tell Juicy to get out.

Juicy pulled over and unlocked the doors. When he turned to Ely with his hand out for the money, he was looking at the pistol pointed at him.

"Is this the thanks I get for letting you walk away?"

"No, you're the one who is going to walk away. Get out!"

"I don't think you've got the guts to pull that trigger."

"Last chance, Juicy. I've got nothing to lose right now. But you do." At that moment Juicy realized, for the first time, he had run out of options. He was always the one making the decisions, telling others what to do. Now he was being told what to do. If he didn't do it, he'd die. Ely would be on the run, Peaches wouldn't say anything, and all his future plans would disappear. Nigel wasn't around to help. He'd underestimated Ely. He hadn't seen the man as a threat. It was a big mistake that would cost him dearly.

"Throw that cannon you're carrying on the floor and step out."

Juicy carefully put his .45 on the floor by the accelerator pedal and backed away. He considered putting his hands up and decided he couldn't do that. It was beneath him to surrender so completely.

"You realize you just signed your own death warrant? And for what: a few hundred dollars? Maybe you should reconsider what you're doing."

Ely reached across the door and pulled it closed, locking it. He slid into the driver's seat and put the vehicle in gear. Before he pulled away, Ely put the window down and yelled, "I think the debt I owed you has just been cancelled. Don't ever try to collect it."

"What are we going to do now?" Peaches asked from the rear seat.

"First I'm dropping you off at the motel. Then I'm heading east."

Ely had gotten his long ride to Jacksonville after all. With all that had just happened, he doubted that he'd be coming back anytime soon, if ever. He didn't like the way the Hummer handled on the highway, but it sure beat walking in the rain.

Back at the motel, Ely had handed Peaches her revolver. "I hope you never have to use this thing. I'm not sure I'd stay here now. If Juicy comes back, he'll want to use your car, or he'll want you to take him somewhere. I'm sorry if I put you in an awkward position," Ely said.

"Honey, I hate to tell you what to do, but Juicy won't ever forget this. He'll come looking for you, and when he finds you, he'll kill you. You do know that, don't you?"

"Yeah, I know. I don't plan on keeping this truck too long. Just long enough to put some miles between us."

"Well, if you ever decide to go back, look me up," Peaches said. "I knew you'd make a good bodyguard. I hope you get whatever it is you're looking for."

Ely couldn't respond to that. Hell, he didn't know what it was he was looking for, but he felt sure he'd recognize it when he saw it.

The rain was coming down harder and driving required all of Ely's attention. He couldn't go more than thirty-five miles an hour and the wind was making the Hummer rock from side to side. The gas gauge indicated a half tank of fuel and Ely was pretty sure the vehicle didn't get good gas mileage. If Juicy reported his Hummer stolen, Ely doubted that anyone would be looking for it in this storm. That bought a few hours of freedom and he took advantage by pulling onto the ramp to Interstate 10 East. He had to make a quick decision: go north on I-65 to Montgomery, which was inland, or stay on I-10 and proceed to Pensacola, which was closer. He decided to remain on I-10 and get rid of the Hummer there. He figured he had enough fuel to get that far.

As Ely approached Pensacola, he saw a young man and woman standing beside a motorcycle, trying to stay dry under an overpass. Ely pulled over, put on the flashers and got out.

"Not good weather for riding that bike," Ely joked.

"You got that right."

"I'll make you a terrific deal. You take my Hummer and give me that Harley you're riding. That way you and your lady friend will stay dry."

"Mister, that Hummer is worth four times what my bike is worth."

"I know, but where I'm going I don't want to show up driving something that's real imposing. My friends will start hitting me up for a loan." It was all Ely could think of as a plausible reason for the trade.

"I don't know; sounds too good. What's the hitch?"

"The hitch is the title is back home under about six feet of water. Take it or leave it, I don't care. It got me out of town, now I don't need it anymore."

"Okay, you got yourself a deal!" The young man's first name was Daniel and he handed over the registration and started to remove all their clothes stuffed into the two saddle bags.

Ely's backpack was in the back and he also needed to transfer his clothes. He had the rear hatch open and noticed a small canvas bag hidden under a blanket. He unzipped the bag to discover it filled with cash. Now he had another problem: trying to stuff everything in the saddle bags. He'd wait until the couple drove off. He had no idea how much cash was in the gym bag, but, knowing Juicy and how he liked to lend money, it had to be a sizeable amount. Ely had left home quickly taking all the money he had stashed away. That amounted to three thousand dollars and change. With the money in the gym bag, Ely could afford to live comfortably, but Juicy would always be searching for him. Now he was doubly glad to be rid of the Hummer.

Ely stuffed the saddle bags, being careful to keep the pistol hidden. The way his luck was running, Ely wondered for a second if the motorcycle might be stolen too. He remained under the overpass, waiting for the rain to let up enough to continue into Pensacola. He noticed the motorcycle had an Alabama license plate; he'd have to remember that in case anyone asked where he was from. The license plate did match the registration and Ely noted that the Harley was ten years old. No wonder Daniel was wearing such a big grin when he drove off.

Ely was familiar with Florida. He knew he couldn't use the coastal route along the Gulf because of the severe weather. Instead, he decided to drop down to Highway 20 and ride east to Tallahassee then Route 27 into Ocala. By then storm conditions should have improved. Meanwhile he rode in light drizzle and was completely soaked. The helmet helped to keep him disguised on the remote chance that Juicy should be following and perhaps even pass him. Stranger things could happen. It had been several years since Ely rode a big bike and it took an hour before he started to relax. He loved the sound of the engine, particularly when he gunned it. For a little while he was feeling completely free.

Ely found a cheap motel just south of Ocala and stayed there for two nights before going on to the east coast by way of Route 40. As soon as he was dry, Ely removed everything from the saddle bags and took over an hour to count the cash. He had $500,000 in various denominations, most of it was in hundreds. He hoped none of it was counterfeit.

Back on the road, he turned south on Highway One at Daytona Beach and discovered thousands of bikers seemingly going nowhere, just hanging around. It was the perfect opportunity to get lost and not be recognized. Ely's only problem was all the motels were sold out for miles surrounding Daytona.

He knew bikers were a friendly bunch and heavy drinkers. It took three visits to different biker bars before he got lucky. Ely discovered a table with four ladies, all in their mid to late fourties. All of the women were admiring him as he surveyed the crowded room. The signaling smiles collided. Ely held up a beer in a friendly salute and they all held up their Margaritas in return. One of the ladies beckoned him to join them, pulling over an extra chair from nowhere.

"You four gorgeous creatures don't look like biker chicks,"

Ely stated before sitting down. "Ooh, if only," one cooed.

"We're down here on vacation."

"Yeah, and we're admiring all the muscle and cute butts."

"Well, I guess this is the place to do it," Ely responded, shocked to hear the ladies talking more like men. They were there to have a good time and so was he. His problem was too many opportunities at once.

"Do you live around here?" one of the ladies asked.

"No, just making a stop-over. I just left New Orleans and Katrina."

"Oh, wow, wasn't that awful?"

"Yeah, I lost just about everything."

"Oh, how terrible for you. So where are you staying?"

"I don't have a clue. I rode over thinking this would be a good place to stay for a few days, never realized how busy it is. Where are you ladies staying?"

"We got lucky and rented a cottage on the beach for a week. We're splitting the rent four ways so it isn't too bad."

"Got a couch I can rent for a few nights?"

"Yes, you bet" and "Certainly" came out simultaneously
with a lot of smiles and giggles.

There were three bedrooms and only one bath. The couch had a lot of miles on it, but it beat some alternatives. Two of the ladies shared a room with twin beds. Ely noticed all of them left their bedroom doors ajar. Everyone except Ely was reluctant to go to bed. In the wee hours, before early daylight, Ely woke to a chorus of snores coming from all directions. One more night would be his limit before heading south. He'd known the minute the four ladies waved their drinks that he'd have a place to spend the night. Now all four were hitting on him in less than subtle ways. They walked to the bathroom to brush their teeth wearing skimpy underwear. One wore a nightshirt and he was pretty sure that was it, nothing else hiding underneath but an invitation.

Ely was amused by his dilemma. Here he was, surrounded by four available women, each eager to get intimate, each trying to best the others, each trying to out-tease the others. Here he was, a thirsty man floating in a sea of saltwater.

Somewhere between the fourth and fifth round of drinks, Ely could vaguely recall one of the ladies mentioning her husband, so apparently they weren't all single.

"Remember what they say about Vegas? What happens in Vegas, stays in Vegas," one of the ladies mentioned.

Ely was enjoying all the flirtation, knowing that absolutely nothing was going to happen in a sexual manner unless all four ladies decided to attack him at the same time. He remembered one of them saying she flew into Daytona from Cincinnati, Ohio, and rented a car, which he later followed to the rental cottage. Sure enough it was on the beach and he could hear the surf when the ladies weren't talking. That didn't stop until around 3:00 A.M. His headache kicked in around 4:00 and dawn showed up around 5:30. He took advantage of the early hour to pee and shower before the ladies started to stir. For an instant, he thought about hiding the toilet paper just to create some hilarity. He pretended he was asleep, listening to the quiet footsteps and whispers. Despite the hangover, he was enjoying this momentary break. The future was out there somewhere and he'd catch up with it soon enough.

Two days later, Ely was on the road again, just like in that Willie Nelson song. He was reasonably rested, took a half hour to say goodbye with lots of hugs, kisses, and promises to keep in touch. All four ladies gave him a phone number to call along with some email addresses. He still didn't know which one was married.

Highway One was his preferred route. He thought about the famous old Route 66 he'd driven numerous times. Every once in a while he'd pass an old motel from the '50s and see the last vestiges of gas stations that once were. The heat increased as he motored south into Melbourne. Mobile home parks and RV parks lined both sides of the highway. Ely slowed down whenever the water appeared. He cut over to A1A so he could see the Atlantic Ocean between the high-rise condos. His temporary destination was Vero Beach. He'd heard numerous people talk about it favorably.

Enjoying the sun and scenery, Ely didn't see a police car sitting in a grove of trees. The next minute he was sitting beside the road with the cruiser, lights flashing, sitting directly behind him.

"Long ride from Alabama, ain't it?" the police officer said.

"Sure is. Most of it was in rain too."

"Okay, let's see your license and registration. Step off the bike, too."

Ely showed the registration the man had given him before driving away in the Hummer.

"Got two different names and addresses here. Help me out with that."

"The driver's license is me. The bike belongs to a guy I know who asked me to deliver it to a guy who wants to buy it. I guess that makes me the delivery boy."

"Uh huh. Are you familiar with the rule of three? That's where the license is from one state, the driver gets stopped in another state and the vehicle is registered in a third and different state. That's what we got here."

"I'll bet you get that a lot down here."

"Yep, it helps pay the hired folks and keeps me busy. Anything in those saddle bags I should know about?"

"A bunch of dirty clothes and my tooth brush. Feel free to take a look."

"Just where is it you're headed to meet this buyer."

"I got an address in Vero Beach. Didn't figure he'd be too hard to find."

"Uh huh. You know anybody down this way? Any family living here?"

"I'll tell you like it is officer. I just escaped Katrina, lost all my shit, and I'm hoping to land a job in Vero once I get there."

"That suggests you are very close to being a vagrant and we've got too many of those already."

The officer had his ticket book out but hadn't written anything. Just then a big truck went zooming by, way over the posted 35 MPH speed limit.

"You just got lucky. That big bastard that just flew by is about to learn an expensive lesson." The officer ran back to his cruiser and sped away. Ely felt instantly relieved. Later, as he passed the officer writing the truck driver a ticket, he honked and waved. The warm air felt good and Ely had a feeling his destiny was just across the next bridge. Instead of continuing on A1A, Ely turned onto Route 510 and crossed the Wabasso Bridge then got back onto Highway One. A sign indicated a small community named Sebastian on the Indian River. The fact that he'd never heard of Sebastian made the place all the more interesting. Juicy would never think to look for him in a quiet place like this.

He stopped for gas and saw a large park across the street. He saw several restaurants with bars on the water and he heard music. It sounded like Jimmy Buffet. He rode beside the water and discovered the source of the music coming from a place called Earl's Hideaway. A long line of motorcycles were parked in a row. The smell of burgers being grilled outside was the final magnetic pull. He was hungry, thirsty, and lonely. All three of these needs would soon be satisfied. For now, this was the end of the road.

Katrina sent him packing, without a definite destination. Ely wanted to remain in a warm climate and not too far away from New Orleans so that he might go back someday, someday when New Orleans was back to normal. Until then, Ely had to settle for an unknown future and follow the road, wherever it took him. It had brought him here to this seemingly quiet place between Melbourne and Vero Beach. A place where hiding out would be less of a challenge. He was already thinking about changing his name when a cute blond plunked down on the stool beside him at the bar.

"Hey handsome, you got a name?"
"Why don't you pick a name for me?"
"Okay, how 'bout Brad? I always liked the name Brad."
"Then Brad it is! What are you drinking?"

Katrina

Katrina, Katrina,
You home-wrecker, you.
Blew off my roof,
Took my pickup truck, too,
The Bayou was home,
After that war
Called Desert Storm,
But you were much more!
Katrina, Katrina,
You broke all the rules,
Broke all the levees,
And left us for fools.

Escaping Katrina

"You want me to do what?" The sheriff shouted into the phone. It didn't take much to make Sheriff Otis angry, and today he was beyond angry. His hand trembled holding the phone and he knew his blood pressure was pegging close to 200. By all accounts, Hurricane Katrina was forecast to hit the mainland within the next few hours and half his men had called in sick or just didn't show up, leaving him shorthanded. He'd been monitoring the storm's path all night.

With limited manpower, he was beside himself, even before this last phone call from some idiot commander with the National Guard. They wanted him to transport the remaining prisoners from Orleans Parish Prison to a temporary compound in Baton Rouge! How did they think he'd manage that? The commander had suggested he use a school bus with as many guards as he thought necessary.

"I reckon yo' all don't realize the situation here, sir. Half my men have taken off, everybody with any sense is trying to evacuate the area. Trying to establish any order right now is simply a joke. So why don't you send down a squad of armed men, along with some adequate transportation, and haul all those sorry asses out of here, 'cause the way I see it, that's the only way they're going anywhere right now. Unless you want me to just release 'em into the general population."

"You can't do that!" the commander yelled.

"Don't be telling me what I can and cannot do. What we have here is a state of emergency, and I'm doin' the best I can with very limited resources and very little patience! Either you send down some troops or I'm opening up all the cells and letting them go before they drown. It's up to you. This just got thrown on me since the warden left town and I don't know who these guys are or what threat they might pose. And I don't have time to figure it out. Some of these guys haven't even had trials yet, and I'm not up for having innocent blood on my hands." With that, Sheriff Otis slammed down the phone.

He knew some of the prisoners weren't hardened criminals, but many of them were. He didn't have time to review their records. Those convicted of murder deserved to die, and drowning was as good a way as any in his opinion. Regardless, he'd have to make a decision soon. People were already crammed into the Super Dome and minor fights were breaking out. Looting would also be a problem. He'd have to patrol some of the flooded areas in boats. He had a call out for help and any available watercraft. So far, no one had volunteered.

"We can't send any troops without the governor's approval," the commander said, calling again to reassure the sheriff that he understood the predicament. The problem was that the governor didn't want to release the National Guard until he heard back from The White House. That begged the question of who was actually in charge. The mayor was busy posing for a TV interview and assuring everyone that the evacuation of the city and surrounding areas was underway in an orderly fashion. The sheriff watched the television screen and muttered to himself about all the stupid statements being made. The mayor didn't have a clue what needed to be done or how to go about doing it, at least as far as he was concerned.

Sheriff Otis had to admit he had limited experience with how to manage a Category Five Hurricane coming directly at him. He was fairly certain the entire levee system would eventually break down, allowing the city to be flooded. In anticipation of the worst possible scenario, Sheriff Otis sent his daughter and granddaughter to Biloxi in his 4-wheel drive Jeep the day before. His ex-wife was already living there. He was waiting to hear from them when the commander's call came through telling him to pack up all the prisoners and be ready to evacuate them.

So now he had to decide what to do. Turn 'em all loose or let them drown? Worry, hypertension, lack of sleep, and way too much coffee was clouding his judgment. If he waited until the very last minute, there was a good chance most of the prisoners would drown anyway. All their records would be ruined or lost before things got back to normal. The courthouse was closed and the electricity was beginning to falter. The television set lost the signal and the lights flickered. The storm was approaching faster than anyone had predicted. Looking out his office window, he could see debris flying by. The wind had picked up noticeably in the past hour.

"Can you believe it, they're turning us loose!" Percy yelled. The pandemonium in the cells was more than a deaf man could tolerate.

A deputy was unlocking all the cells while two other deputies stood by with shotguns, not near enough firepower to hold everyone at bay. They had guts to even be there, Percy gave them that much. Everyone was pushing to get out of the building. Percy waited. If he had enough time, he'd like to sneak into the warden's office and steal his records, just in case they ever started to look for him again. Next time, he might not be as lucky.

Percy was currently serving five-to-ten for grand theft auto. It could have been much worse; they never put it together that he'd also been in on a bank robbery that went bad and a cop had been killed. And they never made him for another dozen B and Es. Now they were letting him go, all because of a damned storm someone called Katrina. Man, he loved that name!

The prisoners dispersed in all directions. Percy's first objective was to change out of his prison garb and into civilian clothes in order to blend in with the milling masses. Nobody was going to give him a lift wearing the bright orange jumpsuit with prisoner printed on the back. As he ran past the sheriff's department a block away, Percy saw a police cruiser parked in the lot. It was like teasing a kid with candy, he just couldn't resist the temptation to borrow it. His luck continued when he discovered the keys in the ignition and the doors unlocked. Later, when he had a few minutes, he'd unlock the shotgun mounted to the dash. The key was no doubt on the ring with the ignition key. *Who'd ever consider stealing a police car?* he thought to himself, then, promptly answered, *Me.*

Percy drove past a dry cleaner & laundry that was closed. He pulled into the adjacent parking lot, left the engine running and smashed the front door glass with the tire iron from the trunk. He grabbed several shirts and slacks, changing behind the counter. He doubted anyone would discover the items missing for a while. The cash register was empty. All he needed now was boots to replace the flip-flops he was still wearing.

Back in the cruiser he found the switch that turned on the roof strobe lights. He made it through two intersections before reaching a long traffic back-up. Horns were honking to no avail; nothing was moving. Percy couldn't afford to be caught sitting in the stolen police cruiser. He found the key to unlock the shotgun. In the glove box he found extra shells. Percy got out, leaving the keys on the seat. Maybe someone else would take it. Traffic remained at a stand-still as he walked alongside stalled vehicles. It appeared most of the residents were fleeing the area and most had chosen this particular route to leave by. Percy had no idea where he was headed. Anyplace was better than where he'd just been.

"Hey, Sheriff, I just saw someone drive off in your car," one of the dispatchers called.

"Damn. He can't get too far. Put out a call, maybe one of our guys will spot it." He remembered he'd left the keys in it thinking he might have to leave quickly. How stupid was that? If any of his officers had done that, he'd have their ass on a plank. And there was a shotgun locked onto the dash that could be unlocked easily enough from a key on his key ring. It was the damned storm; it was driving him crazy!

It hit Percy as ironic: now that he was free, he was still trapped but in a different way. Everyone was outside, carrying personal items, yelling, crying, and acting strange. It was impossible to rob anyone and get away. All he could do was try to blend in while carrying a shotgun at his side. With any luck, he'd spot someone wearing boots his size.

Finding something to eat would be another problem. Maybe the Red Cross would have tents set up somewhere. He didn't like the idea of having to ditch the shotgun, not under the present conditions where a riot could erupt at any moment. Like jail, he didn't feel completely safe, despite the shotgun.

"Okay, Sheriff, we're sending some guardsmen and a small convoy to escort the prisoners back here," the commander said.

"Well, you're about an hour too late, bub. We let 'em all go free 'cause they were about to drown."

"Excuse me, did I hear you just call me bub? Who do you think you're talking to?"

"Right 'bout now, I'd say I'm speaking with an idiot. You don't have a clue how bad things are here. Your troops will sure enough have a hard time getting here, so you might as well use 'em to stuff sandbags where you are. Too late to do any good here. And, you can tell the governor I think he's a first-class asshole, too." *And that goes for you, too,* he thought.

"I'm going to report you for this insubordination. They'll have your badge!"

"Yeah, you do that. Talk to the mayor while you're at it. Right now he's busy giving a television interview to CNN. It's the best he's looked in ages with all that make-up on."

"Who's there to relieve you of your authority? You're obviously losing it, Sheriff."

"That's the first thing you've said makes any sense." Sheriff Otis slammed down the phone and walked out of his office, put on his tan Stetson, and walked into the downpour.

He had no idea where he was going, but he had to get away from the damned phones and all the stupidity. He was due to retire soon and wished now he'd taken an early retirement when it was suggested. He hoped the commander's blood pressure was as high as his. "Let him bust a gut," he muttered to himself as he walked across the parking lot in ankle-deep water. Anyone watching would see the sheriff carrying on a conversation with himself and wonder about his mental state.

"You seeing what I'm lookin' at?" the dispatcher said to the one remaining deputy who was about to leave. "I think Sheriff Otis is losing it. Look at him, standing out there in the rain, in the middle of that intersection, like he was directing traffic."

"Yeah," the deputy said, "only there ain't no traffic! I better go get him before he gets in trouble."

He'd overheard pieces of the recent phone conversations with Baton Rouge and thought the sheriff had some balls standing up to those fools.

Channel 7 News happened to have a news crew, along with a cameraman, shooting local scenes when they came upon the sheriff, standing in the intersection, waving his arms and yelling. They recognized him wearing his telltale Stetson. They got it all on tape.

"Looks like Otis has left the building," the cameraman said, zooming in on the sheriff. They needed humor to get through this tragic event that was unfolding before the lens. He noticed a deputy running toward the sheriff in the rain. The deputy was trying to pull the sheriff away from the intersection and the sheriff seemed to be resisting. Both almost fell.

"What do you suppose that's all about?" the driver of the news van asked. He pulled up and stopped directly in front of the two police officers.

"Get the hell away from me!" Sheriff Otis yelled, motioning to the oncoming van to stop.

"Sheriff, they need you inside right now!" the deputy yelled to make himself heard above the howling wind. He still had the sheriff's left arm.

"Nobody needs me, nobody will listen to me. I'm quitting, as of right now. Here, take this badge and put it on. I'm authorizing you to be the acting sheriff. I gotta find my damned car and get the hell out of here." He had to get home, get in bed, and get some sleep. He hadn't slept in the last forty-eight hours. He'd finished off three pots of coffee during the night and the next morning of the storm, refusing to take a drink of liquor. That took some self-control. Otis was so wired his hands shook. Then, while standing in the rain, he felt the growing pressure between his temples suddenly explode. Earlier, he'd attributed his headache to tension and high blood pressure.

National television coverage of Katrina ran a brief clip of the sheriff directing ghost traffic in a downpour. They didn't show the segment where the sheriff tore off his badge and later collapsed into the waiting arms of a deputy as if he'd been shot. The crew called 911, knowing it might be an hour before any medical attention arrived. It was already too late.

In reality, Sheriff Otis escaped the storm with a massive aneurism in his brain. It had been coming before Katrina hit.

Four blocks away, the news crew caught up with a crowd of looters. Standing in the road, in the middle of the crowd, Percy was seen holding a shotgun. In the next second, someone fired a shot and Percy fell to the street, still holding the gun. Viewers would never know he'd just been released from prison less than an hour before. Nobody cared.

Saturday Morning Blues

Saturday mornings we were always busy at the 12th Street Mission. Homeless people from all over the city seemed to congregate, check in with one another. Mostly they were glad to see their friends, know they were still okay, and enjoy a few laughs despite their sad situation. There was always plenty of coffee.

This Saturday we ran out of oatmeal first then pancake mix. As a replacement, we served scrambled eggs and sausage for as long as the sausage lasted. By 9:30 we ran out and had to resort to making French toast with leftover stale bread. Our larder was running thin and someone had to make a run over to the food bank. Those of us who volunteered at the mission took turns going across town to replenish our dwindling stock. More and more, we were running short on Saturdays because of the increased numbers stopping by. I didn't know if it was because of the declining economy or if we had simply become popular.

Some of the faces and names you remember, seeing them often.

Rudy was a perfect example; he only showed up on Saturday mornings. The rest of the week he must have haunted a different shelter. Like many of the visitors, Rudy was a street person whose age could have been fifty, or it could have been closer to sixty-five. Nobody knew. Nobody cared. Like a lot of things, it just didn't matter. Many of the mission's guests didn't seem to know if it was Monday or Saturday. Sometimes, because we were so busy, I couldn't tell either. Mondays used to be quiet by comparison, but recently that had changed. So

Mondays could easily be the same as Saturday, with some of the same visitors.

Leave it to Vinny, one of the regulars to ask, "Hey Rudy, when's your birthday?"

"Why?"

"Well, I thought maybe we could, ya know, throw you a party or something."

"I'll tell you the same thing I told you last time you asked: it's none of your damned business. So don't ask me again!" Rudy was gruff, but he didn't appear to be upset. Everyone knew Vinny was a 'nosey sumbitch.'

"Well ex-cuse meee. What happened, somebody pee in your wine bottle last night? Hah, ha, hah." This seemed to get everyone's attention.

"Ya wanna know about last night? I'll tell you about last night. I had a date with a very nice lady, and, in fact, we did share some wine."

"Get ripped on some Ripple, did ya?"

"I don't recall what it was; didn't matter 'cause we shared it."

"Uh huh, did you spend the night with her? Or was this another one of your romantic dreams?"

"None of your damned business! But you should be so lucky, Vinny."

"This lady got a name? Maybe I know her. Maybe she was in one of my dreams, too. Hoo, hoo, whooo."

"Yes, she has a name, and I'm not giving out that information. She wouldn't appreciate me talking about her."

"Ooooh, sounds serious. You spend the night in her sleeping bag or yours? Oh wait, I forgot, you don't have a sleeping bag."

That digging remark caused me to wonder just where Rudy spent his nights. Most of the shelters had limited capacity causing most homeless people to find places under overpasses, in large cardboard boxes, sometimes in a doorway or in an abandoned vehicle. None of those choices was desirable, but, should it rain, they were better than a park bench.

"Actually, we layed out on the grass in the park and watched all the stars overhead. Without any moon, the stars were really bright last night. It was nice. Nobody bothered us. If there had been some music, we might have danced, not that it's any of your business," Rudy said with a grin. A few heads nodded in agreement. I had the feeling Rudy was making all this up, just to put Vinny on.

"Well, ain't that special. I'm surprised the cops didn't show up and run the both of you off for loitering, and maybe for whatever else you were doing."

Vinny's last remark got a few laughs. Most everyone there knew he liked to agitate Rudy. It occurred to me that Vinny liked to agitate a lot of our guests.

He particularly liked to pick on Ben. We usually called him 'Big Ben' because he was 6'4" and had to weigh close to 300 pounds. We fondly called him "Big" leaving off the "Ben." He always wore bib-overalls and looked just like the big old farmer he once was. He was from the upper Mid-West somewhere. If you asked him a question, his best friend, Jake, would usually provide the answer. That's because Big had a low I.Q. and didn't talk much. When he did, it was almost stilted, never conversational.

What made this twosome so interesting was while Ben really was big, Jake was short, close to 5'6", with a slight build. The contrast reminded me of the two characters in the old classic movie *Of Mice and Men* when I saw them together. Like all the rest of our guests, nobody used a last name, only first names, some of which were street names.

Like Jump. Jump was a nervous guy who never sat still. He moved in a jerky sort of way. His face twitched too. And he laughed at everything, causing others to laugh as well. Only his was a nervous laugh.

Rudy was on his third cup of coffee and moved to another picnic table to avoid Vinny's ongoing barrage of personal questions. It wasn't just Rudy he picked on. He'd focus on anyone, strike up a casual conversation and slowly try to penetrate that person's background. Sometimes they'd respond, but I doubted what any of them said was true. The exception might be Big. He didn't lie or stretch the truth. He said what he felt in simple terms. Big sat next to Jake as they were finishing their breakfast of French toast. As usual, Big was working on a second helping.

"I wish they had pancakes. I like pancakes," Big said to Jake.

I recalled several weeks back when we were celebrating Big's 40th birthday. We served him a plate stacked with five huge pancakes. On top we put a lit candle and everyone sang happy birthday. I remember seeing tears form in Big's eyes. Then he quietly announced, "I think I did this once before. I was 40 then, too." Apparently Jake misinformed us, but it didn't matter. The fact that he had a candle to blow out pleased him, as it would any six or seven-year old kid.

"Can I have some more orange juice?" Big asked Jake.

"Sure, I'll see if they have any more in the kitchen," Jake said getting up.

"Hey, Jake, you should probably bring out the jug and let him drink from that," Vinny yelled across the room. Jump thought that was hilarious, standing up and clapping his hands together.

"Don't call him Jake! His name is Jacob!" Big announced.

"Well, pardon me, but I wasn't speaking to you."

"I don't like you!" Big said, looking directly at Vinny.

"Yeah, well live with it, kid. Let's see, Jake rhymes with snake, maybe that's what I should start calling him, Jake the Snake. Hah, ha, hah."

"Stop! Don't say bad things about my friend."

"Yeah, or what?"

"I make you hurt bad!"

All other table conversation had stopped. Everyone heard the exchange. It was the most we'd ever heard from Big, probably because Jake was still in the kitchen, looking for the orange juice.

"Listen up, people, the giant here just threatened me." Vinny had a big smirk on his face. He loved playing to an audience. He was standing on the bench so he could tower over everyone present.

Jake returned with a paper cup of juice, handing it to Big who had gotten up from his seat. It looked as if he might walk over to Vinny, and everyone was holding their breath. It was rare to have any commotion this early in the day, regardless of the day. Evenings were different. The drunks could be rowdy. The morning crowd might suffer a few hangovers from the night before, but rarely did they make a fuss.

"Cool it, Big," Jake said patting Big's shoulder to calm him down.

"I want to go now," Big announced turning to the entrance.

"Okay, everyone have a good day," Jake said walking behind Big.

"Not him! I don't want him to have a good day!" Big said leaving.

"Hear that? He tried to put a hex on me," Vinny cackled.

The room remained quiet for a full minute while everyone contemplated what had just transpired. With Jake's help, Big managed to control his temper.

"Hey, Vickie, read any good books lately?" Vinny asked, having spotted another target. He must have felt the need to fill the recent void.

Vickie looked to be in her early to mid-fifties. Her gray hair looked a bit wild. She reminded me of an old hippie. Whenever I saw her, she always appeared neat. Someone said she had a part-time job at the Salvation Army outlet. It was a good place to get nice, used clothes and, working there, she'd have her pick of the better items. Sometimes Vickie helped in the kitchen when we were short-handed. Mostly she was just quiet and you didn't realize she was there.

"No, I lost my library card," she responded to Rudy's question.

"I can give you one; I have several. People keep losing them and I keep finding them at the library. But it will cost you a kiss."

"Ugh, I'd rather kiss a pig! You're sure you aren't stealing them?"

"Hey, don't paint me with that brush. Just because I don't turn them in doesn't mean I'm a thief. I was just offering you one to be nice." Rudy was still playing to an audience, smirking and lifting his eyebrows up and down.

"You should turn them in. I can get a replacement the next time I'm over that way. Funny, I haven't seen you there."

"That's because he spends all his time in the bathroom,"

someone commented, followed by a few giggles in the audience.

"I go there to read the newspapers," Vinny responded. He was one of those people who liked to dish it out to others but didn't take it too well when he was on the receiving end. Given an opening, several of the guests were quick to jump in with a zing.

"Yeah, he's searching for his obituary," one of them said. More snickers.

"That would make for some interesting reading," someone offered.

"Can't have an obituary unless you have a last name," Vickie said.

"Yeah? Well I got a last name, I just can't remember it right now. It's because the IRS is after me. I owe back taxes for the last fifteen years."

"You ain't worked in the last fifteen years," someone replied.

"Well, go figure. Maybe it's child support for my ten kids then."

Everyone laughed at that and Vinny felt he'd had the last word.

I was on duty as a volunteer the next Saturday and was keeping busy clearing the tables, throwing out trash, mostly paper plates, plates without any food left. It didn't get wasted at the mission. All the coffee, creamers, and sugars were donated by a coffee service company headquartered in New Orleans. Once the expiration date hit, they could no longer sell those products, so they donated them to homeless shelters. The products were still good. The creamers were all powdered, not in liquid form. I thought it was a wonderful gesture and made sure every local business in the neighborhood knew about it. Consequently, a local bakery started giving us their day-old bread for toast and sandwiches. A local supermarket agreed to give us paper plates, cups, and napkins. Sometimes they'd also provide us with bacon and sausage when the expiration date was getting close and they couldn't sell it.

The noise level seemed lower this particular Saturday, then I realized why: Vinny wasn't there. Mooch was the first one to mention it.

And neither were Big Ben and his buddy, Jake. Certain visitors stand out and you remember them. When they didn't come in for their Saturday morning breakfast, I began to worry. Maybe they'd moved on. I knew some homeless people were like nomads, drifting from place to place. They would cluster for a while in one spot, like a park, then move on when the police, sometimes with a show of force, urged them. Rarely did such conflicts make the news, but we saw the results when they showed up at the mission. Lots of dirty bandages and bruises. I felt sorry for them. I understood their need to lie and make up stories. They lived one day at a time, not thinking about a future.

"Anyone seen or heard from Vinny?" I asked.

I saw a lot of heads shake, *no*. Nobody seemed concerned except me.

Maybe he got picked up by the police. After all, these were homeless people who lived on the streets and in the parks where anything could happen to them. Getting arrested was actually a good thing because then they had a safe place to sleep, they could shower and get fed. Sometimes they got medical help.

Another week passed and Vinny seemed to have disappeared. Nobody reported seeing him which was strange because most of the homeless people in this section of town knew who he was. They knew him for being nosey and loud, for asking too many personal questions that nobody ever wanted to answer.

If he was dead, I knew there wouldn't be any obituary and that hit me as a sad fact. Nobody knew if he was a veteran or not. Maybe he'd been awarded a medal for valor somewhere. And somewhere he had an estranged family who may have given up looking for him. If he was dead, somebody needed to play taps on a trumpet, if for no other reason than to commemorate a life as a human being who had suffered the indignities of mankind. Like him or not, he'd be missed. He did, after all, add a bit of entertainment.

Strangely, we never had another visit from Big and Jake either. They had parted the mission on a rather awkward note. I remembered that Big did not want Vinny to have a good day.

And maybe he'd made that bad day happen. I'd have to wait to find out. Maybe it was better not to know. Sometimes I felt like a person feeding a stray animal who visits your back doorstep for a handout. They show up for a few days and eventually disappear, moving on. You think about them and wish them well. It's all you can do, because they never let you get attached to them.

12th Street Shelter Blues

"Let me tell you about homeless people. They got nowhere to go and all day to get there," Herman said to a small audience. He sat at a picnic table drinking coffee and telling stories. Some of them were jokes; all of them were true.

This was at a shelter on 12th Street, where the homeless could get a hot meal and stay warm on a cold evening until closing time. A local church sponsored the program and church members provided the help necessary to run the place. I was one of the volunteers. Whenever I saw Herman, I always tried to spend a few minutes with him in conversation because he was so funny. He made me, and everyone around him, laugh.

The 12th Street Shelter occupied a small storefront in a neighborhood that had fallen on hard times. The building had been vacant too long. Next door was a laundromat where the homeless could do their laundry. Only about half the machines worked. We supplied the quarters for the machines and the free coffee while they waited. The church operated this particular storefront which was open for breakfast at 7:00 every morning offering hot oatmeal, cold cereal, hot biscuits, gravy, and hot coffee. A local bakery donated day-old bread that hadn't sold. Lunch was soup. Sometimes it was a simple tomato soup, other times we got creative and made chicken noodle soup, with lots of noodles and not too much chicken. Carrots helped to add some color to the concoction. People on diets, trying to lose weight, will tell you hot broth is good for you. We used that as our guide. It was always served with a smile and grateful responses were abundant. That was my reward.

"I know a homeless old lady who cuts out coupons and sells them to people on welfare," Herman said to no one in particular. When nobody responded, he went on, "Now you take me, I'm so poor I don't even qualify for welfare."

"That's because you don't got no last name," somebody yelled out. Everyone laughed at that, including Herman.

"That's true enough. When you lose your last name, you ain't got much else to lose 'cept a few teeth. But the law now, they get all bothered by that. They got to have a last name else they can't put you in jail."

"Sure they can. They just don't want to 'cause we all smell so bad." The group was getting into it now, chuckling, laughing, and enjoying each other's company before taking on the outside world. They arrived cold and hungry and left with a meal in their belly and a laugh or two to start their day.

The pastor arrived and announced to all present, "Anybody want to work today? I've got several openings for some manual labor."

"Man, you realize when they say 'manual' they mean hard work? How much they paying?"

"They're paying seven dollars an hour and it includes a free lunch. They'll pick you up out front at eight sharp," the pastor said.

"Shee-it, seven dollars is slave wages. I don't know if I'm willing to be used like that. I got twenty-five dollars yesterday for giving some of my blood. Now they want me to sweat some more of it for seven dollars. Won't have much blood left in me. What I need is a job sitting down, telling other people what to do."

"Herman, you got something better to do today?" I asked.

"Man, anything's better than working. My new main hobby is sitting around the park watching the pigeons poop on everything. I think those pigeons are all reincarnated homeless people come back for revenge."

"Herman, you're the leader here. If you show up outside for work, the others will follow you."

"Yeah, and blame me for all their aches and pains the next day, too. I got a better idea. How 'bout I collect a dollar from each of them for being the leader. You know, like the unions do."

"The unions provide some benefits. What will you be providing?"

"What I always provide: entertainment. I make people laugh, even when I ain't very funny. It's my smile that gets 'em." He cocked his head and gave me that silly grin. It worked.

We called Zeke our watchdog. He'd spend the entire morning sitting on the bench outside the front door nodding to those who passed by, like the greeters at Wal-Mart. He'd wave to the passing automobiles and sometimes you'd hear them toot their horn. He'd become somewhat of a permanent fixture sitting there drinking coffee.

Sometimes people stopped to ask a question or for directions. It occurred to me that we should probably give him a tin cup to hold while he was out there nodding and waving.

That thought was confirmed when Zeke said, "You won't believe what some nice old lady just gave me." He'd just come in for another cup of coffee. He proudly held up a five-dollar bill. "That's the most anyone has given me in quite some time. Mostly they just give a dolla'."

It suddenly hit me that people were giving donations, meant for the shelter, thinking Zeke represented us. No wonder he parked his buns outside the entrance every day.

"Just how much have you collected sitting out there like a cigar store Indian?" I asked.

"I ain't no Indian! I'm an American, and I'm a veteran, too."

He'd missed my point. "Zeke, if people stop by the shelter and donate money, they're doing it to help run the shelter, and you sitting outside the door, well, they naturally think you work here. They don't mean for that money to go to you. It's for the shelter."

"How do you know that? Nobody ever told me I couldn't keep that money. I'm the only one sitting out there all day. You should be paying me to do that."

"I'm suggesting that you do the right thing, Zeke. The church doesn't have much money and what little it has goes to support this shelter. You benefit from that. Look at all the free coffee you drink here."

"Okay, take the five. Next thing you'll be telling me I owe you rent for the bench."

"Not a bad idea considering how well it has worked out for you." Now I knew why he never stood outside in the work line.

By 9:00 the shelter was almost empty. Lubelle was one of the homeless women who liked to help out in the kitchen. When everyone was gone, she'd wipe off the tables before sweeping the floor. She was a big woman in every aspect, including her heart. She reminded me of Aunt Jemima on the pancake boxes and syrup bottles. She had the very same broad smile.

"So what are your plans for today?" I asked.

"You mean after I get my hair and nails done? I might go shopping. I hear the dumpster behind the new Mexican restaurant has interesting discards. They use those clear plastic trash bags—makes it easier to see what's inside."

"Now don't go off on me, Lubelle, but just how do you manage to get yourself into a dumpster?"

"It ain't all that easy when you're as big as I am. But I know where they keep the stepladder. That's my secret. Now don't be blabbin' it about, hear?"

"Your secret is safe with me. Just be careful you don't fall."

"Which way? Into or out of the dumpster?" Then she gave me that high-pitched wail of hers. She could easily sing in a soul-based choir. A few minutes passed and another woman I'd never seen before entered. She was very cautious, taking in the room and sparse furnishings. The picnic tables worked better than tables and chairs.

"It's okay, Ruth, you can come on in and sit down anywhere. I'll get you a cup of coffee and I saved you a few biscuits," Lubelle said.

"Welcome to the Twelfth Street Shelter," I said. "If you don't mind, we'd like for you to sign in on that clipboard hanging by the door. Just a first name is okay. We like to know how many people have visited us each day. That's our way of keeping a count." I felt it necessary to explain because she seemed so nervous.

"Can I put down any name or do you want my real name?"

"Put down whichever you prefer. Lubelle said your name was Ruth."

"I go by a lot of names, depending on where I am at the time. Lubelle changed her name, too, did you know that?"

"I changed it from Lubella 'cause I thought it sounded like one of those diseases you don't want to ever catch," Lubelle said defensively.

"Who you show that list to?" Ruth asked.

"Well, it hangs there for anybody to see. Is there something you're afraid of, Ruth?"

"Oh, you bet! I'm especially afraid of the cold. I'm also afraid of the white kids that come around at night trying to beat on us and chase us off. The police won't do nothin' 'bout it. And I'm afraid of the police. You can't trust 'em. They chased me out of the park once and called me names."

"Where do you sleep?" I asked.

"Lubelle and me, we got us an old Chevy station wagon that don't run. Some of the windows is cracked, but they still keep out the rain and we can crank 'em down a little when it gets too hot, which ain't too often."

"So you're living in an abandoned car."

"Can't be abandoned if we're living in it. It's our home. We took out the seats and put down pieces of cardboard on the floor. Not too many homes got five doors to get outside."

I was trying to imagine it, two women, one big as a house, the other frail and thin, both sleeping in an old car parked somewhere. With the doors locked, they'd be safer than sleeping on park benches or in a cardboard box. Even a tent.

While Ruth was using the bathroom, Lubelle whispered to me, "She's afraid of everything. Her ex-husband beat on her pretty bad before she finally got up enough nerve to do something."

"She finally left him?"

"No, she finally killed him! Waited until he fell asleep and put a knife into him. She's been hiding out ever since."

"How long ago was this?"

"'bout ten years ago. Now don't be telling anyone about it. She's a nice lady and didn't deserve to be hurt like that. She's been paying for what she did every day since then."

"It's good that you look after her, Lubelle."

"Yeah, we're friends. We keep each other company. Sometimes I have to make up stories so I got something to talk about."

"Why not tell her real stories about yourself?"

"Honey, it's just too sad, and I don't want to think about growing up so poor like we were. I put all that out of my mind a long time ago, and I don't want to go back for a visit, no, no. It just hurts too much to even think 'bout it."

I thought back to when I was a kid growing up. I guess we were poor, too, but I never gave it any real thought. It certainly wasn't a bad period, and I didn't have any negative feelings.

As if reading my mind, Lubelle asked, "When you were young, did Santa Clause come visit your home?"

"Yes, he always came while I was asleep."

"Uh huh, and did he leave something in your stocking? Something nice, just for you?"

"Sure. Usually it was candy or an apple and maybe a small toy. One year it was a yo-yo." I could still remember that Christmas as if it was yesterday. It was a happy time even though we didn't have much.

"See how lucky you were! Santa never visited our house; never! I been putting up a stocking for thirty-two years, and he ain't never come by!" I saw her wipe away a small tear, then she smiled again.

I thought how sad that was. If I had anything to do about it, this next Christmas Lubelle would have a big surprise waiting. I'd fill that big stocking of hers with all the candy it would hold.

Maybe I'd add some assorted snacks as well. Sooner or later I'd learn where that old Chevy was parked. I made a mental note not to forget because it was a high priority item now. It was something I wanted to do.

I had a few hours to kill before the lunch crowd arrived so I walked to the library to read a few out of town newspapers, like the *Washington Post*, *USA Today*, and the *New York Times*. I'm no longer interested in politics, even though it surrounds me daily. I'm more interested in things like the world's sliding economy and how all the strife in other countries seems to come about, because humanity won't recognize the problems under its nose. It's greed, not compassion, that's the primary motivator for rulers everywhere.

On the other hand I think the Peace Corps has done more good than any of our big funding that somehow never gets to where it is needed. I'm thinking of Haiti and its recent disaster. The money gets lost or stolen. The food and clothes never find their way to their intended and the starving people just get their picture taken for CNN. How frustrating it must be to witness all that as a missionary working there.

What those people needed was someone like Herman and Lubelle. In my opinion, they'd make great missionaries. They understood suffering and knew how to overcome minor discomforts. They knew how to survive. In no time, Herman would have them all laughing and Lubelle would have them singing and smiling.

Thinking about Herman, I realized that he'd become sort of a daily fixture at the shelter. I always looked forward to seeing him. He took a small slice of light and passed it my way, making me all the richer for having known him. He viewed life as a simple man with simple needs and laughed at his plight, challenging all that he feared. Humor was his armor and it served him well. It was a lesson I needed to learn and use.

Herman made a difference in my life as well as others. He made a hard life look easy. He didn't have a last name, and he wasn't included in the last census. He didn't even have a library card or a wallet to carry it in. He never spoke of a family or his past. If he had regrets, he never showed that side either. It would take a long time to really know him…if he stayed around long enough. Ask too many questions, and many faded away to another temporary place, so I knew I had to be careful.

My reward for volunteering was to witness the human condition up close and as personal as it could possibly get. These were needy people the world did not want to acknowledge. It made me feel humble to be among them.